2232

Ken Kroes

Edited by EditorNancy/Fiverr.com
Cover Design: SelfPubBookCovers.com/RLSather
Book design by Ken Kroes

ISBN: 978-0-9940332-2-2

Publisher 1779671 Alberta Inc.

This book is a work of fiction. Names, characters, places, and incidents either are products of the author's imagination or are used fictitiously. Any resemblance to actual persons, living or dead, events, or locales is entirely coincidental.

For more information please visit my website www.the2222book.com

CONTENTS

1 ENIGMAS

Lauren flicked a switch and changed the frequency of the base radio in the computer hut. "Come in, Port Aspire. This is Lauren over at Percipience."

After a brief pause, an official deep sounding voice could be heard. "This is the director of Cannabis Operations at Port Aspire."

Lauren rolled her eyes and shook her head. "Hi Clyde, um…I mean Director. Have you seen my husband lately?"

"Hey Lauren! No, I haven't seen the man around. I think he's off working on his special project."

"Well, when you see him, please have him radio down here. I've got a huge surprise for him."

"Why not tell me? I'll get the message to him."

"I want to tell him myself. I want to hear him come completely unglued when he hears about what we've found over here." She said as she looked again at the WISE monitor in disbelief.

"Well, suit yourself. The next time I have a secret, I'm not sharing it with you! But since I'm such a nice guy, I'll get in touch with the man and give him your message."

After she signed off of the radio, Lauren spoke to the people who worked on the WISE system and told them that if anyone called for her, to come get her from the classroom over at the Research Lab.

She then looked up at the clock realizing that with the excitement in the computer hut she had lost track of time. *I'm going to be late.*

We know, we're all here already, came the instant response from her class.

She smiled as she quickly left the computer hut, quite proud of the progress that her current class was making.

For the last decade, with the help of the genetic data processor, the percentage of children that showed psychic powers had increased considerably. Lauren took it upon herself to hold classes in both Percipience and Port Aspire to help the older kids learn to focus their abilities. Telepathy, extra sensory perception and telekinesis were the most common abilities. Those that showed exceptional psychic powers were given the opportunity to join an advanced team that was also led by Lauren.

As she exited the computer hut, Lauren found her four-year-old daughter just where she left her, sitting cross-legged on the ground. She had made a series of concentric circles in the dirt with a stick and had some stones placed on the circles and seemed to be in deep concentration. "Come along, Heather," Lauren said. "Mommy has to go and work with her class while you go visit with your Grandpa."

Heather's large pale blue eyes displayed her excitement at the mention of her grandpa. She jumped up, straightened out her long curly hair and followed Lauren over to the Research Center.

Though Lauren, Alec, Heather and her two brothers, Logan and Lucas, lived in Port Aspire, Lauren made the journey to Percipience once per week to spend time with her family and her team and to host her psychic classes. Heather joined her on most of these trips and developed a great fondness for her granddad, Robert.

"Hi Lauren. How's my favorite granddaughter?" Robert said as they entered his lab.

"Dad! You're not going to believe what we found out on WISE!"

"What?"

"I'm super late for my class; I'll tell you and Alec together as soon as he calls back. Can you watch over Heather for a bit?"

"Jeremy too!" Heather interrupted.

Everyone who knew Heather, knew about her imaginary friend Jeremy, as she included him in everything that she did. "Yes, of course, I won't forget about your friend Jeremy," Robert said as he reached down to pick her up while motioning to Lauren that it was ok for her to leave.

Lauren entered the classroom that was right beside her dad's research lab. The room itself had a simple layout consisting of a series of tables and chairs that were currently facing the presentation area. One side of the room had windows with a view out into the forest while the rest were lined with blackboards, all full of equations and notes from other lectures and workshops.

Though there were about twenty kids in the room when Lauren entered, it was dead silent. *OK, everyone, time to come back to the real world and start speaking out loud.*

"We can't start yet, we're missing five kids," one of the students said.

"No, they're not missing. I asked them not to come back," Lauren said.

"Why?" came the response from several shocked kids.

"Though they had some psychic abilities, they were not very strong at it."

"That's not fair. They were trying."

"I'm not here to build up false self-esteem. To progress and stay in this group, it doesn't matter how hard you try; what matters are results. Now, what happened to you?" Lauren asked one of her students who had fresh bandages covering her nose.

"Well, I wasn't paying attention," the eight-year-old girl said. "I was in a telepathic group chat with some friends and ended up walking straight into a tree."

This brought a mild chorus of laughter from the rest of the class.

Lauren brought the class back under control and started the morning lessons, which were related to singling out a person in a group telepathically and also putting up a shield so that someone could not connect with you. To do this, she taught them the game of telepathy tag.

The class was getting the hang of the game; soon, a new person was tagged as "it" every second or so. Suddenly, Lauren received a subconscious signal from the "Hive," the nickname of a collection of ten of the strongest telepath's who subconsciously monitored for any nearby negative thoughts against Percipience or Port Aspire.

The warning left as quickly as it appeared as one of the other Hive members took care of the threat. When a threat was detected, one or more members of the Hive focused thoughts towards the source to divert thoughts of violence and anger to some other, happier thought. This counterattack from the Hive increased in intensity until the threat to the village or any of its residents disappeared.

Lauren looked at her sons Logan and Lucas who were in her class. Logan, her eldest, looked back. *Yes, I got that one,* he sent while not missing a beat in the tag game. Lauren was very proud of him; though he was only nine, he showed great psychic strength already. His brother was good but had not yet shown the same potential. The one that Lauren was really curious and also worried about was Heather. Though still too young for her class,

Lauren could tell that her daughter's psychic skills were unmatched. The thing that unnerved Lauren was that Heather *knew* things, things that were not possible to be known. Not just what people thought or their emotions, not past or future events, but *how* thing worked. She was the only child that Lauren had ever met that never asked, "Why?"

****

Alec took a long drink of cold water as he reviewed the morning's progress made on his current project, one that would finally connect Percipience to Port Aspire.

Ten years had gone by since the confrontation with Epoch, Allison, and his father. During this time, Alec and a few hundred other people from both Percipience and Epoch had worked to build up the coastal expansion village, Port Aspire. The name of the village was determined through a contest, won by Clyde, who later revealed that it was a clever anagram.

During this ten-year period, Alec gained a deep appreciation of the amount of effort that had gone into building the original villages like Percipience. The plan for Port Aspire was to replicate much of the layout of Percipience but on a smaller scale. Even with this reduced size, they had so far only managed to build a fraction of the buildings and supporting infrastructure.

The goal for Port Aspire would be a slightly smaller self-sufficient village and it would not have the full manufacturing and research capabilities that Percipience had. Instead, Port Aspire would concentrate on building electronic components, computer chips, lasers, and memory devices from the information in WISE and the elder's library. Port Aspire would then supply these electronic components to Percipience and its sister village in Australia named Provenance. In exchange, Percipience and Provenance would do some of the metal and woodworking manufacturing for Port Aspire.

Of course, these were all future plans as Port Aspire was still getting the basics in place. Also, even though there was a great deal of radio communication with Provenance, there was no trading at all between it and either Percipience or Port Aspire. In fact there had not been a single trip yet made to the southern hemisphere village.

Port Aspire was about one hundred miles south of Percipience and it took about a week to go between the villages by foot with a light load. The more common way was to take the twenty-hour barge trip along the coast and then up river to Percipience. The barge made the round trip twice per week, which worked well for transporting food and other items, but was far too slow for effective collaboration between the two villages.

Flying helped some for moving people and small items for the first several years; however, a few years ago there was a large fight between Alec and Jordan resulting in Jordan and Kimberly leaving Port Aspire to return to Epoch, taking the plane with them. The dam that was along the roadway between Epoch and Percipience had also completely failed, so all three villages now were in isolation from one another.

To build another plane would require more effort than Alec could spare, so he decided to build an airship that could carry a large payload instead. Alec's plan was to power the airship with a cold fusion reactor and to use excess heat from the reactor to heat up the air in the balloon. After adding a couple of uniquely shaped propellers, the plan was for the ship to be able to make the trip to Percipience within a few hours.

Alec's break was interrupted by a squawk from the radio. "Alec, hey man, you out there?"

Alec recognized the voice. "Hey Clyde. I'm here; what's up?"

"Your wife called for you a bit ago. Something about some big surprise she wanted to tell you about but she wouldn't tell me. Can you imagine that? I question your judgment at marrying someone like that!"

"Well, I can't change that," Alec replied. "I'm done here for today anyhow and need to get to my regular work. I'll be there soon."

Alec did one last review of his project. With the help of a few others from

Port Aspire, the cockpit and general seating area were done. The next steps were to build the detachable cargo area and the ribs for the envelope, the large balloon-like structure that made up the majority of the craft. Due to the massive completed size, the construction site for it was on a hill on the far side of a hemp field that was on the edge of Port Aspire.

Though there was no air chair yet installed anywhere in Port Aspire, the poles and cables were in place for it. Alec grabbed his backpack and climbed up the air chair platform that was beside the construction site. From atop of the platform, he could see across the hemp field, the trees between it, the partially completed village and finally the ocean. He had selected this location for the village due mostly to the flat terrain and the perfect ocean cove that had gentle waters, even during the worst of storms.

Reaching into his backpack, he pulled out a harness with a special clip that he had designed. Putting on the harness and then attaching a clip to the air chair cable, he stepped off of the platform and was soon gliding down the cable. The scenic trip took only a few minutes versus the nearly half hour walk to the village center.

Alec detached himself from the cable and walked over to office in the partially completed town center where he and Clyde called up Percipience. It took a couple of minutes for Lauren to get to the radio. "Alec, I have my dad here as well and both of you are not going to believe this!"

"What's going on?" Alec replied.

"Well, you know how the WISE system has started to ask random riddles and questions at times. Guess what question came up this morning."

Alec looked at Clyde who shrugged his shoulders. "We have no idea."

"It asked how many treasures are in the pyramid. The operator brought me in when WISE didn't accept the number 'two' as an answer."

"Okay," Alec said, his interest now piqued.

"Not knowing what else to do, I had the operator enter in 'three,' and that was the right answer!"

"No way! How could we have left something else behind?"

"Well, get you butt down here so we can go and check it out!"

2 QUESTIONS

Epoch Times March 30, 2232

Following last month's startup of Epoch's first radio and television broadcast stations, this weekend will mark the opening of the first electronic store in our city. "Everyone now can enjoy the free radio and television broadcasting that has been tested during the last month," Dave Supersell said. Dave is the manager of the new store and has been working closely with the city to get the technology online and available. "We now have five radio stations and two television stations. Most of the content is from before the Great Loss but there will be local news and time set aside for any local groups. The opening of this store is the culmination of years of work in the design and manufacturing of the broadcasting equipment and to cheaply provide devices for the public to use. We have also teamed up with Epoch's bank to arrange for financing for those consumers that just can't wait to have these in their homes."

****

The Commander of the DC watched as the soldier nervously stood in front of his desk during the prolonged silence that followed the report he had given on his last mission.

"There was no way that we could do it." The soldier blurted out, not being able to handle the silence any longer. "It is hard to explain, but the closer we got, the more wrong the mission felt."

His commander nodded his head. He had heard the same story from previous missions that he had sent up to Percipience to exact revenge for the horrible act that they committed on Epoch a decade ago. *I'm sure that witch Lauren has something to do with this. There must be some way to get to them.*

The commander dismissed the young man and sat alone in his office at the DC. Anger built up inside of him as he reflected on how things could have been if only Robert had not done that despicable act. *Robert was not the only one to blame though. Alec must've known about this and could have put a stop to it or at least have warned Epoch. But I'll not give up; their action demands retribution and I'll make sure that it happens.*

Just then there was a knock on his door and Kimberly came in. She and Allison had been at the DC all morning training on the usage of the new night vision goggles they had developed at the Re-Discovery Center.

"Hi darling. Allison still has work to do but I'm all done. Did you want to go and grab a bite to eat?"

"Not right now," Jordan answered abruptly. "I have work that needs to get done right away and then I have a presentation to give downtown."

"Can't you take even an hour off?"

"No, I can't. This presentation is too important. I'll be home late tonight too," was Jordan's crisp response. Kimberly recognized the now too familiar tone and realized that there was no room for negotiation.

"OK, I'll see you then," she said while leaving Jordan to brood in his office.

Initially after the confrontation with Percipience, Jordan was excited about the new life that he and Kimberly were building for themselves in Port Aspire. Then one night on a visit to Epoch, he had more than a couple of beers with Jake and found out the truth about what happened at Epoch. Robert had poisoned the water resulting in the sterilization of the town. Jordan reflected on how things would have worked out if this had not happened and how he would have been the head of Percipience and probably Port Aspire as well.

When Jordan returned to Port Aspire, he talked about Robert's actions with Alec and was shocked to find out that Alec already knew of Robert's actions and actually defended them. This triggered a huge argument resulting in Jordan taking Kimberly and the plane back to Epoch. Upon his permanent return, Jake appointed Jordan as commander of the military of Epoch on the condition that Jordan did not mount a retaliation attack on Percipience or Port Aspire.

As the years passed, Jordan's anger did not go away but festered and grew stronger instead. Without Jake's knowledge, Jordan did make a few attempts to attack Percipience. All, including this recent attempt, had ended in failure.

There was another knock on his door.

"I said I was busy!" Jordan said in an elevated voice.

"Yikes, sorry," Allison said as she came in and closed the door behind her.

At the sight of Allison, Jordan relaxed considerably. She was the one person who seemed to understand the pressure he was under. She was also the one person who agreed that Percipience needed to pay for its actions.

"No, I'm the one that's sorry. I thought you were Kimberly. She was here a little while ago and wanted to go take me out for lunch even though she knows I have this big presentation coming up later today." Jordan stretched his neck by moving his head side to side. "I also just got word that our last attempt against Percipience failed."

"That's horrible," Allison said as she moved behind him and gave him a shoulder rub. "But don't give up. Robert, his daughter, and the rest of that horrible village need to be taught a lesson."

"At least you understand." Jordan reached up and put his hand on Allison's. "We're recovering from the setback that they inflicted and could easily take them out if only I had Jake's approval. But he wants nothing to do with them and is concentrating on our expansion to the south."

Since his arrival at Epoch, most of Jordan's responsibilities focused on building bigger planes—ones with wheels instead of pontoons—and landing strips while managing the increasing air fleet with flights down south to other smaller villages. After the confrontation, Jake put effort into getting couples from other small communities from the south to move up to Epoch, giving people that moved large incentives and even larger ones once they arrived if they had large families. The strategy seemed to have paid off; in the last decade, a couple thousand children had been born.

"So, are you going to starve yourself? I was thinking of getting a bite to eat myself."

"I'd love to but I need to meet with Jake and give a presentation in an hour or so. Did you need a ride back to Epoch?"

"Sure; I think Kimberly forgot about me. I saw her car leave with a fair amount of speed."

Jordan put on his dress military jacket.

"You'll do great at the presentation." Allison said approvingly as she did the final touches on his jacket to make him look perfect.

On their way out of the command building, they stopped off at the computer room so Jordan could check the shift schedule. In the room were two terminals connected to a single computer and there walls were lined with data discs. Going over to the abandoned Asia village that had been setup a few hundred years ago by the Pleasant Belief Foundation had been Jordan's idea. Remembering the location from the map in the pyramid, he coordinated the logistics of flying over there, finding the local pyramid, and acquiring the WISE system from it for Epoch. When the computer system was up and running in Epoch, he then told Jake about it and he was ecstatic. Both agreed that though no longer necessary, they would keep a small team up in Percipience under the guise of doing WISE research; really, they were just keeping an eye on what was going on.

****

"Sorry for leaving you at the DC. I was so upset with Jordan that I wasn't thinking straight," Kimberly said as Allison came into the lab after lunch. "How did you get back?"

"No problem. I got a ride," Allison said and then quickly changed the subject. "Did those micro boards come back from the fab shop yet?"

For the last ten years, Jake had the priority of the Re-Discovery Center set to electronics. With ample books and with the help of WISE, there was quick progress in making the basics of monitors and simple integrated circuits, which formed the basics for broadcasting equipment, televisions, and radios. The current projects centered on military applications, such as night vision goggles and radar as well as civilian communication devices like cell phones.

"Yes they did," Kimberly said. "I was starting to hook things up so that we can test out this mini microphone and transmitter. Why is Jordan being like this? He's so absorbed in all of this military stuff."

"He's the commander of our DC! That's a huge responsibility," Allison exclaimed. "In addition to that, Jake has left it up to him to supervise design and construction of the new air fleet and landing strips that they need. That's more than a full-time job on its own."

"I know, but he just doesn't talk to me anymore. I have a feeling that he's up to something, and Jake is probably involved." Kimberly was interrupted by a series of beeps that were coming from an instrument in the back of the lab. She walked over to it, jotted down some numbers, and then hit some buttons to run another variation of the test just performed.

Kimberly studied her note pad as she walked back to Allison and then tossed it onto the lab bench. *How can these numbers be so high?*

"You are still playing with the emissions controls for the refinery aren't you?" Allison asked. "You know that Jake would flip out if he found out you're doing this. Pollution control isn't on the approved projects list."

"I'm doing this mostly on my own time. This doesn't impact anything at all except for giving us some cleaner air. The CO2 scrubbers I made at Percipience for our refinery are working, or at least they were working. I can't tell anymore since I can't seem to get any decent readings out of that damn machine back there."

"Is it really that important? It's just one little refinery and we're not the ones who get to pick the priority on what we work on anyhow. We don't have all of the information that Jake has to make the decisions on what we should work on next. Right now it's all about electronics," Allison said while wondering why Kimberly was wasting time and not concentrating on important things like research that would help Epoch grow or on supporting Jordan.

****

Jake stood at the podium in a small conference room at the city town hall and pressed a button to bring up the next image on the overhead screen. The screen listed a series of medicines, electronics, and other commodities.

"This, gentlemen, is a partial list of what Epoch has to offer your villages as part of a trade agreement that would be part of the alliance we can form. Many of these items took us years to develop with our sizeable research staff. Having access to them will put you decades ahead of where you'd be if you were on your own."

The audience paid close attention both to the projected list and to the words that Jake was saying. They were a collection of the representatives from small villages to the south of Epoch that had been found through aerial reconnaissance. This meeting was setup to discuss the signing of an alliance between themselves and Epoch, which included an ongoing trade agreement. Conspicuously absent were any of Epoch's elected officials who had simply delegated the entire negotiation process to Jake and only wanted to be involved in the signing ceremony.

"In addition to trade, Epoch will provide both television and radio signals to your villages, providing both news and entertainment to your citizens. Of course, one of the biggest advantages to the alliance would be the protection and security that Epoch's military can provide."

As if on cue, Jordan entered the conference room from the back and strode with purpose up to the podium.

"Ah, here he is now," Jake said gesturing towards Jordan. "Everyone, if you have not met him yet, this is Epoch's military commander. He's going to go over the defense capabilities of Epoch and how we can utilize these to protect your villages as well."

Jordan thanked Jake and then took his position at the front of the room and spent the next hour going over the growing size of the air fleet, weapons, and men that he had at his disposal. He outlined the levels of protection, law enforcement, training, and regular air transportation that could be provided to each village. The final part of his presentation covered the landing strips and buildings that would be setup at each location, at Epoch's expense.

"Thanks Jordan," Jake said as he retook the position in front of the group. "So that's the end of my proposal. In short, military protection, trade between us, air transportation and a common currency to facilitate things. In return, Epoch will receive a small tax from all of you which will be more than offset by the increased commerce that you'll see. I'll let you discuss this amongst yourselves and sleep on it. Tomorrow, if you're all in agreement, we'll have the formal signing ceremony for the formation of the Fair Alliance Region."

There was a rousing applause and handshaking as Jake thanked his guests then headed out of the room towards his office. "How'd you think it went? Do you think they'll agree?" Jordan asked as he tried to keep up with Jake's brisk pace.

"I'm so confident that I've already had the new currency printed," Jake said as he sat down at his desk and reached into a drawer pulling out a crisp new bill and handed it to Jordan. He then pulled out two glasses and poured a shot of brandy in each, handing one to Jordan. "Here's to the new Alliance and an end to the current currency notes from the Bank for Universal Regional Payments."

"Thanks," Jordan said as he took a sip while examining the new bills. He read the banner on the bills and immediately took another, bigger gulp to help him from not laughing out loud. *Fair Alliance Region Treasury. God, I know what the common abbreviation of these will be.*

After Jordan left, Jake looked at his desk and specifically the stacks of paper he had to review that had accumulated over the last few days. *Most of this is due to the elected officials who demand constant reports without considering the amount of effort involved in maintaining them. Soon though, after the Fair Alliance Region is formed, I'll deal with them too.*

3 RIVALRY AND DISCOVERY

Kimberly was relaxed at the controls as she guided the small float plane to a smooth landing by Percipience. She regularly did the supply flight but was surprised when Allison asked to join her on this trip since she had not been back to Percipience since the big confrontation ten years ago. After docking the plane, she and Allison headed up to the village site to get their research team to help in moving the supplies from the plane and to pick up their research notes.

"I need to go up the Research Center and use the washroom," Kimberly said as she left Allison to help the local team transfer the supplies.

When she reached the Research Center, she looked behind her to make sure she was not being watched and then detoured over to the lab entrance. She was glad to find Robert there.

"Hi Robert. I don't have a lot of time, but I'm wondering if you could look this over for me." Kimberly reached into her inside jacket pocket and pulled out an envelope.

Robert's face lit up when he saw Kimberly. He had missed chatting and working with her. "Sure, what's this all about?"

"Sorry, I don't have time to explain. Jordan will get angry if he finds out that I've spoken to you at all, and especially on this topic. I'll get in touch later to discuss. Please don't try to contact me," Kimberly said nervously as she quickly left the lab.

****

Lauren and Heather watched the plane land from the dock as the barge came in with Alec and Clyde. They were heading up to the computer hut when a Hive warning came up from Lauren's subconscious. There was a strong threat and it was very close by. Lauren expanded her psychic field and immediately pinpointed the source. Looking in the direction of the Epoch Cabin, she saw Allison who was standing at the doorway and looking directly at her.

Lauren sent a message to the Hive that she would handle the situation and entered the computer hut with Heather.

Allison kept thinking that she was finally over everything that happened here ten years ago but just the sight of Alec, Lauren, and their daughter brought everything back like it was yesterday. *She has the man and family that should have been mine.*

In the time following the confrontation, Allison had several boyfriends but nothing felt anywhere close to how it had been with Alec and she longed so much to feel that way again. *It's all her fault.*

The only person that really understood her pain was Jordan. They had spent many hours planning attacks against Percipience even though Jake had explicitly said that they were not to. She knew that Jordan liked her a great deal and she could feel her nerve endings tingle each time they "accidently" touched one another. But he was spoken for, even though Kimberly did not appreciate how much stress he was under. *Kimberly does not know how lucky she is.*

Allison noticed the cute curls in Heather's hair. *If I hurt Lauren, then I'll be hurting her. No, this is wrong. I need to be focusing more on Jordan. If Kimberly does not love him, then maybe there's an opportunity for me.*

Kimberly returned from the Research Center and Allison felt somewhat guilty for her latest thoughts, though deep down she knew that they were true. Shaking her head slightly to clear her mind, she continued on with the supply transfer.

Lauren was sitting down near the WISE terminal when the subconscious

Hive message came in that there was no longer a threat. The whole exchange from the initial detection of the threat to the all-clear had taken only a few seconds. *I didn't realize that Allison's anger still ran so deep. The Hive will have to be extra vigilant from now on.*

"Do you have any idea where we're going to start looking when we get to the pyramid?" Lauren asked Alec as they sat in the computer hut with Clyde. There were no operators from Epoch working, allowing them to speak freely.

"No clue really," Alec said. "We scoured the top floor really well on our second trip up there. I'm guessing that whatever it is should be on the lower floor, but there was so little in that room."

"Did you wise guys think of asking WISE?" Clyde asked, quite proud of his little play on words. He turned his chair to face the second terminal.

Alec and Lauren looked at each other and shrugged their shoulders. "Why not?"

Clyde pulled up the search page and typed in "Third Pyramid Puzzle" and clicked the search icon.

Several results were displayed but it was obvious that the top link was the right choice. "Power, wisdom—what else could there be?"

Clyde selected the link and was surprised that there was no prompt for a data disc. Instead, a soft chuckle came through the speaker. "You must have encountered the riddle question on this. I am not going to make it too tough but I need to make you work a little bit for the third surprise," the soft-spoken voice of Richard said. The screen then showed the following;

yfh mvwcpidypvi bvx yfh yfpxs auxgxpah pa yehiyj yev yfpxyj yev

"Huh?" Alec said, and then looked at Lauren who shrugged her shoulders. "What's that? Is it broken?"

Clyde stared at the string of letters for a moment then smiled followed by a quick flick of a switch to turn off the monitor. "We must head off to the pyramid right away!"

"Why? What did that gibberish mean?" Lauren asked.

"Duh, like I'm going to tell either of you," Clyde said pointing to his forehead. "This is my ticket to a trip out to the pyramid. I've never been there and I'm not going to miss out on it this time."

"Lauren, could you do a little mind magic on him and get him to cough up what he knows?" Alec asked.

"Sure, it would probably leave him as a zombie though."

Clyde looked at both of them a little afraid until he realized that they were playing with him. "Nice try. Let's go and get the big guy's approval to head out."

The trio stopped off at the lab and found Robert jotting down readings from an instrument on the lab bench. As soon as he noticed the intrusion, he quickly turned off the instrument and picked up a piece of paper, placing it in his pocket.

"So, are all of you ready to try and solve this third puzzle?" he asked.

"Been there. Done that," Clyde said.

"So he says," Alec said gesturing towards Clyde. "We did a search on WISE and found a cryptic message. Clyde claims he's figured it out but won't tell us. He is essentially blackmailing us so that we'll have to take him on the trip. Anyhow, we're planning on heading out there tomorrow morning, and since Logan and Lucas are up here visiting anyway, we were thinking of taking the kids with us." He then looked directly at Heather. "Including of course, Heather's friend, Jeremy."

"I'll be coming too," Robert said. "I've been racking my mind on what else could be up there and where."

Spending the rest of the afternoon in preparation, Alec, his family, Robert, and Clyde headed out the following morning. To speed up the trip, Heather took turns riding on Alec, Clyde, and Robert's shoulders.

They were nearly at Little Bear Lake when Clyde tapped Alec on the arm and pointed up. Alec looked and saw a cloud formation in the detailed shape of a rabbit contrasted against the blue sky.

"Is that yours?" Alec asked Heather.

"It was Jeremy's idea."

Another small set of clouds formed and quickly organized into the shape of a snake that was slithering towards the rabbit cloud.

"Logan! Stop it!" Heather screamed at her brother as the snake prepared to strike.

"Just playing with you," Logan said as the snake morphed into the shape of a carrot, which brought shrieks of laughter from Heather.

"Another typical day with your family," Clyde said shaking his head.

After camp was setup at Little Bear Lake and the evening meal was completed, the kids spent some time around the fire listening to stories from Lauren about the wolves and specifically about her wolf. He had passed away several years ago and though Lauren's relationship with the cubs from his pack was close, they were not at the same level.

Alec walked up to Robert who was sitting on the ground, drawing and making notes in his notepad.

"What are you working on?"

"A new problem. One dealing with greenhouse gases."

"What's the problem beyond the fact that there's too much?"

"I'm not positive yet, but there seems to be even more than there should be. But enough of this for tonight; I'm going to get some sleep."

With most of the group having never been to the pyramid before, the camp awoke early with eager anticipation and arrived at the pyramid shortly before noon. There was a fair bit of plant growth on the old lake bottom but the structure did not seem to have aged at all. The white marble sides were remarkably clean and the golden top glistened in the sun.

The kids dashed ahead to explore the structure.

"OK Clyde, time to tell us what the message on the computer was all about," Alec said.

"Well, it's pretty easy actually, and that's why I turned off the terminal so quickly. It wouldn't have taken you too long to figure out that it was a simple letter substitution message and translated to, 'The combination for the third surprise is twenty-two thirty-two.'"

"With the dials?" Alec asked and then walked over to one of them, fully expecting it to be set to the number two for the first combination they entered. To his surprise, they were all reset back to the initial position.

"Must have happened when we found the bottom floor. I know that I didn't go back and check these," Lauren said.

With the assistance of Logan and Lucas, it did not take long to enter the 2232 combination and soon they felt a rumble underneath their feet.

Adults and kids scurried around the pyramid and through both floors but could not find anything that had changed.

As they sat outside of the structure, exhausted from their search, Robert said, "We all felt the ground tremble. Something happened."

It was Lucas who noticed it first. "Look," he said pointing to the cap of the pyramid. The cap was now above the main structure, supported by four bars. There was a foot wide gap between it and the pyramid structure.

Lucas went up to the base of the pyramid and felt the marble surface. "How are we going to get up there? This surface is super smooth and steep. There's no way we can climb it all the way to the top, which has got to be at least fifty feet high."

"Can't one of you fly up there or something?" Clyde asked.

Lauren turned and gave him a disapproving stare. "You do realize that it's taking me more energy to hold back from turning you into a zombie than it would take to make you one."

After about a half an hour of ideas being suggested and shot down, Clyde stood up. "What would you guys do without me?" He then motioned Robert and Alec to come with him. They returned a short while later carrying a log that they found along the edge of the creek. Placing the log on the wall, Clyde started to crawl up while Robert and Alec held it steady. The tree reached to within a few feet of the top and soon Clyde was looking into the gap between the pyramid and its golden top.

"What's up there?" Alec called out.

Clyde did not say anything, and after ten minutes, he started to head back down, clinging to the tree with all of his strength. When he finally got to the bottom, his face was white. "I guess I'm not that good with heights, but I did find this up there." He then reached into his shirt and pulled out a plastic case containing two data discs.

After spending the evening at the pyramid and telling stories to their children of their first discoveries there, the group moved quickly the following day, making it all the way back to Percipience by nightfall. During the journey back, they all took guesses as to what was on the disc.

"An anti-aging drug would be nice," Robert said as he shuffled Heather, who was sitting on his shoulders.

"How about an anti-gravity machine?" Logan suggested.

"A weather machine, maybe?" Lucas said.

"A teleportation device would be nice," Alec said.

"Knowing Richard and his fondness for riddles, I'm guessing that it is full of riddles that will take us years to solve," Alec said.

Though tired when they arrived at Percipience, they went straight to the computer hut and were relieved to find the Epoch team was again not there.

"Where are they? " Lauren said. "I haven't seen them for quite a while."

"We can look into that later," Clyde said. "Right now let's find out what's on these discs."

They mounted the first disc and turned the computer on. Within a minute, an unusual picture came on the screen that seemed to show some kind of machine.

"Ah, very good," the familiar voice of Richard came from the computer. "This third and final surprise I think you'll really make use of. On these discs are the plans and operating instructions for a machine that manufactures nanotube materials. Ultra-light and ultra-strong, I can just imagine the uses you'll think of for them. Not only can the machine make various sizes of rods, it can be configured to make nanotube planks, pipes, and even nanotube fabric. You may be wondering why I did not unveil the machine when the villages were first formed. The reason is simple—there really was no need for it then. Now, what should be roughly two hundred years later is when you'll probably really need it, perhaps to start a new village."

As Richard spoke, the image on the screen was replaced with a picture of a cable not much bigger than a thread supporting a one-ton weight and then a video of a piece of fabric that could not be pierced with a bullet.

Alec looked at some of the specifications of the new material and did some rough math on a notepad. "We have got to build this machine right away! I've got the perfect use for it," he said.

Excited about their discovery but tired, everyone left the computer hut. That is, everyone but Robert. He was tired as well, but he needed to do one thing before he could get any sleep. He pulled up a chair to a WISE terminal. Over the years, he had graduated to a two-finger typist and it did not take him too long anymore to find what he wanted, though in this case he wished that he had not.

The numbers on the screen and the readings that he took a few days ago confirmed his rough calculations and also what was in the letter from Kimberly. He turned off the computer and headed back to his clan hut. Tired as he was, he was certain that he would not be getting any sleep this evening.

Robert,

I hope things are going well for you and I do miss the time we used to work together. I'm hoping that you can find some time to help me either find the error that I'm encountering or confirm what I'm afraid may be true. I've refined the CO_2 scrubbers for the factory and I think they are working well, but when I try to measure their efficiency, I'm having issues with getting the level of CO_2 in the normal atmosphere, away from the factory. I'm getting readings that are in the neighborhood of 650 ppm, which is much higher than before the Great Loss. This should not be possible but I've measured it several different ways now, and I keep getting the same results.

If this is all checks out, I fear we may have runaway greenhouse gas emissions where the resulting heat from the emissions causes even more emissions to be released, probably from the permafrost areas in the far north. I hope that you can find an error in my logic.

Also, Jordan will be horribly upset if he finds out that we are communicating, so please don't send me anything. I'll stop by in a few weeks and hopefully I will have more time to talk to you about it then.

Regards,

Kimberly

4 PLANS

From his office in the DC, Jordan and Allison were examining a map of the area around Percipience while he described his latest plan. "Do you think it'll work?"

"It's ingenious," Allison said in soft and approving tone while looking directly into his eyes. "It avoids us attacking Percipience or Port Aspire directly but the impact, at least to Percipience, will be devastating."

"There are so many ways to make them pay. The whole trick is to avoid the Hive," Jordan said.

"Right. I was curious as to how the Hive worked, so I went up there on the last resupply mission. There I had a first-hand encounter with it when I saw Alec, Lauren, and their daughter walking together. For a moment I thought of the pain that you and I will inflict upon them. Within a second, however, I really didn't want to think about it anymore. It was kind of like thinking of hurting a cute puppy; there was no way that I could imagine myself doing it and I started to think about other things. On the return flight to Epoch, after we were about fifty miles away, I started to feel normal again and the thought of attacking them didn't bother me at all."

Jordan listened intently. "I've never experienced it myself, but every soldier I've sent out there reports back pretty much the same encounter that you did. What did you start to think about instead? Several have reported thoughts of people or things that they cared deeply about."

Allison hesitated for a moment. "The same for me. The anger was replaced with another thought," she said as she reached across his desk and put her hand hesitantly on his. "I thought of you."

Jordan turned his hand over and gently caressed hers. Allison's nerves tingled throughout her body as they looked into each other's eyes. "I think of you often, as well," Jordan said. Then after a prolonged pause, he added,

"But right now I need to concentrate on my job. Jake has been relentless in his demands for getting things setup quickly for the Alliance. If that fails, then none of this," he squeezed her hand gently, "will matter."

Allison nodded. "Well, then let's get at things. It'll take me quite a while to secretly make the amount of chemicals that you're going to need for this. When were you planning to do it?"

"Could you have enough ready in six months? There are some other supplies that I need to quietly acquire as well and I'll need that amount of time to do so."

Allison thought for a moment. "Yeah, six months should be doable. Everything else has to be planned perfectly, and you already have a great deal on your plate. Let me know if there's anything that I can do to help," she said as she gave his hand an affectionate squeeze.

After Allison left, Jordan thought for a few more minutes about her and then stood up to clear his head. He glanced at the clock on the wall and realized that he was late, again, for dinner.

****

Alec and Clyde were heading back to Percipience's town center to meet up with Robert after a full day at the fabrication hub where they had been helping building two nanotube machines: one for Percipience and the other for Port Aspire. With several people interested in seeing how or even if the machine worked, there was lots of help, and Alec thought it would only take two more months to finish building the first few prototypes.

They found Robert in the radio room chatting with Aaron, the lead elder at Provenance, one of the four initial villages built by the Pleasant Belief Foundation in Australia. Though Robert and Aaron had communicated for years over the radio, they had never met.

Robert learned through Aaron that Provenance was about half the size of

Percipience primarily due to the extreme weather and the difficulty in growing enough food. Due to this, most of the new information exchange between the villages had been one way, from Percipience to Provenance. Other than size, the two villages were quite similar with both still following the original guidelines set out by Richard.

Robert was wrapping up telling Aaron about their find at the Pyramid.

"After entering in the combination and a bunch of searching, we finally noticed that the gold top of the pyramid had risen above the rest of the structure. There was a struggle to get up to the top, but once there, we found the plans for a machine that makes nanotube technology."

"Nanotube technology? What's that?" Aaron asked.

"I didn't know either until a week ago when I looked it up on WISE. Apparently ultra-light and ultra-strong, this material can be used to build nearly anything, and all from common natural resources and a pile of energy. With the cold fusion reactors though, energy isn't a problem, so we're going to try it out. I have some people building a couple of these machines right now, and it just so happens that two of them have just joined me in the radio room."

Alec and Clyde pulled up chairs close to the radio speaker.

"Hmm…interesting that there's no mention of nanotube technology in the Elder's Library," Aaron said.

"Yes, that's curious. Must have been another one of Richard's secret projects," Robert replied.

"And this was in the top of the pyramid? Like you, we thought that there were only two surprises in there," Aaron said. "We're pretty busy right now and a bit short on people, but I'll try to spare a few to get back there and get those discs. Keep us updated on the machines you're building."

"What's this Elder's Library he mentioned?" Clyde asked.

"There's a small library of books in the Elder's room," Alec said. "When I became the lead elder at Port Aspire, I was introduced to it and was told that the books were mostly related to future technology that Percipience was not ready for yet—things that would be useful mostly when there were more villages. I skimmed through the books but don't recall seeing anything on nanotube technology either."

"What kind of books are in there?"

"A fair bit on electronics. Things like integrated circuits, lasers, and magnetic mediums. Also a fair bit on astronomy and astrophysics."

"If we're planning on building electronics at Port Aspire, maybe we should get a few of those books," Clyde said. "Robert, would you mind if I took some back to read? WISE is nice for finding quick answers but nothing beats reading through subjects in a book."

Robert agreed so Alec and Clyde left for the Elder's room to take a look at the library while Robert concluded his call with Aaron. When he was done and with the radio turned off, Robert leaned back in his chair. Something was bugging him about the conversation that he had with Aaron. *Ah! That's it. How did Aaron know that the plans on the top of the pyramid were on data disc or that there was more than one? I never told him that.*

****

Kimberly waved to her nanny who was crossing the street in front of her car. *Great, this means that Jordan must be home from work.*

With this bit of information, Kimberly switched her turn indicator and turned away from her home and drove down the road that led out of Epoch and towards the DC. Once there, she reached into her glove box and put a few items into her purse before entering the main office building. Being late in the day, it was quiet in the building with only a single guard at the front desk. He was intently watching a television program from before the Great Loss, some type of competition with people eating bugs.

Kimberly approached the desk. "The commander forgot some papers in his office and asked me to pick them up on my way home."

The guard recognized Kimberly and waved her through and then went back to watching the television where a man was crunching through a live spider.

Once in Jordan's office, she went over to the television monitor that had been installed only recently, slipped off a side panel, and with a small screwdriver made short work of installing an extra bit of electronic hardware.

The whole operation from start to finish took only a couple of minutes and the guard barely acknowledged her as she left the building. *Jake and Jordan are up to something and maybe now I'll find out what. The microphone and recorder that I installed will get power from the television, even if it is turned off, and will record up to two weeks of conversations that I can retrieve and listen to.*

5 MELTDOWN

Epoch Times – April 13, 2232

This upcoming weekend will mark six weeks since the he formation of the Fair Alliance Region joining Epoch with four other communities to the south. Already, there has been a marked increase in trade between the cities and overall plans are ahead of schedule; however, it appears that several of the elected officials from Epoch have decided to take personal advantage of the alliance. This paper has obtained copies of documents showing that companies owned by several officials are getting preferential treatment in the trade agreement. These companies not only are getting more than their fair share of the business but at prices higher than their competitors.

During an interview with Epoch's city manager, he indicated that he has been in touch with the other villages to ensure that they understand that he will get to the bottom of the issue and make sure that they're treated fairly. As to how this happened, he could only speculate since the city office that he runs had provided volumes of reports to the officials indicating the imbalance right from the start of the agreement.

****

Jordan got up and turned the television in his office off after watching the evening news with Jake. The program included an interview with Jake discussing the current scandal around Epoch's elected officials.

"Do you think I looked convincing enough?" Jake asked.

"Heck yes. Completely believable. The interviews with some of the other elected officials have them coming across as fools."

"Good. I'm having the television station concentrate on this story for quite a while. We'll make this the number one thing that people are concerned with and talking about. That's the big advantage of the media and why I pushed for its re-discovery and then deployment through Epoch and the rest of the Alliance."

"I can see the advantages clearly. I'm assuming you're putting some influence in to have the same coverage at the newspaper?"

"Of course, and after a few months of this, I'll be able to put the next phase of my plan into action."

"Which is?"

Jake smiled. "That's my secret for now. But I'll tell you this: It'll change the government here forever and both you and I'll benefit greatly!"

****

Over his entire time as lead elder of Percipience, Robert tried to follow the guidelines that were set out when the village was initially formed. This included doing his part in the regular rotation of chores and work that were needed to keep the village running. Over the last few days, however, the problem that he was investigating seemed important enough to use his authority to delegate his normal work and to commandeer Percipience's time on the WISE terminal.

He knew that the current greenhouse gas levels were much higher than they should be. But even with the information available in WISE, he could not tell for sure why this was. The most likely cause was the release of methane from the permafrost regions in the far north as the Earth grew warmer, but there were several other possibilities as well.

What concerned Robert more was the impact that these elevated gases were having on the planet, and what he found brought him grave concern. The last data point for CO2 levels in WISE was nearing 450 ppm from the year 2020, and the world at that time was already experiencing some extreme climate change.

With current levels of 650 ppm, the predictions were for planet-scale changes with an estimate of a four-degree temperature increase. This increase in temperature would result in widespread draughts, super hurricanes and cyclones, major extinctions of species, and sea levels rising twenty or more feet. All in all, it seemed pretty grim.

With Percipience being fairly isolated, Robert did not know if these predictions were coming true or not, but he did know from Aaron that the conditions in Australia were pretty dire. With the extreme weather they were experiencing, they could not rely on outdoor crops anymore and so they grew most of their food in greenhouses.

The one small piece of good news in all of this was the location of Percipience. The combination of ocean currents, jet streams, and the Rocky Mountains to the east resulted in a sweet spot; the village was spared the worst of the conditions, at least for now.

It's no excuse, though. Even though we're not too impacted now, we should have paid more attention to this earlier. We've grown too complacent in our little world.

****

Why were they doing this? How long has this been going on? These questions and several more were swirling through Kimberly's mind as she wiped away the tears while listening to a recording from Jordan's office. The recording was from late in the afternoon a few days ago. A day that Jordan came home very late because he said he had an extended staff meeting and then a pile of paperwork.

Kimberly had finished fast-forwarding through the recording of the meeting and was about to skip to the next day's recording when she heard a knock on the recording, a door open, then close and then a soft click. *Was that the door being locked?* She immediately recognized the female voice of the person entering.

"Hi, hun. How was your meeting?" Allison asked.

"Ended early," Jordan replied, "which was perfect since our dinner delivery arrived just as it was finishing."

"Yum. I'm starving," Allison said. "I stayed late at the Rediscovery Center waiting for Kimberly to leave so that I had some time to work on getting stuff ready for our project."

There was a pause in the conversation and a couple of sounds that Kimberly could not quite make out.

"How's the thermite coming along?" Allison asked.

"Fine, all on schedule," Jordan said followed by the rustling of bags as they were obviously unpacking the dinner.

"Do you have to go home soon?" Allison asked.

"No. I told her that I'd be very late since I had meetings and then a pile of paperwork."

"Perfect. I'll do my part to make sure that you're not a liar by ensuring that you come home very late."

Kimberly could only listen to a small portion more of the recording before turning it off.

6 CHANGES

Epoch Times – July 2, 2032

With the scandal of the elected officials now finally behind us and the offending officials ousted, the election for new members is now in full swing with Election Day just three months away. In addition to the usual candidates running for the positions, there is an unusual twist. For the first time ever our city manager is running, but not as a single council member; he is running to replace the entire council himself. To win, he will need to get a super majority of the vote, at least 80%, but recent polls have him higher than that. The question is if he can hold onto that popularity for the three month election campaign.

****

Heather entered her clan hut with a string in her hand that was attached to a floating cylinder.

"Where did you get that?" Lauren asked, examining the peculiar floating object. Heather had shown some telekinetic abilities but this was her strongest showing by far.

Lauren pushed the cylinder down but it slowly rose again as if it was buoyant. "How are you doing that?" she asked as she was not able to detect any psychic activity from her daughter.

"Doing what?"

"Making the cylinder float."

"I'm not doing anything, Mommy. Daddy gave it to me and Jeremy."

Lauren headed over to the fabrication hub where she found Alec leaning over one of the nanotube machine prototypes that he had brought from Percipience a few weeks ago.

"I take it Heather showed you the little present that I gave her?"

"How did you make it float? It looks like it is made out of that nanotube fabric."

"Yes, you're right. The machine works! I've been able to make small sections of cable, planks, and as you've seen, fabric. I'm making some adjustments to it so we'll be able to run any size we want."

"But how did you make the cylinder float?"

"I've been thinking of that toy since I was a kid in school. Basically anything can be a balloon as long as the object is lighter than the volume of air that it takes up. Usually balloons contain hot air or a gas that's lighter than air, but I've always wondered if I could build one using a vacuum. The problem has always been that any material used to make the balloon itself is either too weak to handle the pressure or too heavy."

Lauren looked puzzled as she thought through what Alec said. "And all of this nanotube stuff is strong enough that it doesn't get crushed?"

"Exactly, and it is super lightweight, so if you make an object out of it and then make a vacuum inside, it floats. What I gave to Heather was a test; I have much bigger plans in mind." He put his hand around her waist and after an affectionate kiss, led her over to a drafting table. "Basically I'm going to build a long tube with this stuff and then setup a frame made up of nanotubes inside to work like a big accordion."

Lauren noticed the dimensions on the drawings. "These are huge—three hundred feet long and three feet in diameter. What would you do with one of these?"

"Not with one; try about *fifty* of them. They're going to be what lifts up the airship that I'm making. With some intricate mechanics and the accordion design, I'll be able to precisely control how big each one is and I'll not have to worry about filling the thing up with hot air or using a gas like hydrogen or helium. It can take off on a moment's notice."

"So how long until the whole thing is complete?"

"There's a lot of fabric to make and then all of the supporting rods and planks. It'll probably take a few months or so before I'm completely finished. With the calculations that I've done, I can afford to cover all of the tubes and mechanics with a nanotube fabric exterior too so that it'll still look like a real airship and have a cargo capacity of several tons. The cover will also allow someone to look at or fix the mechanical stuff controlling the tubes without being exposed to the elements or wind."

Lauren snuggled closer to Alec and gave him a kiss on the cheek as they both looked at the plans. "That's brilliant." Lauren could not help but notice how vibrant Alec's mind was. It was one of the qualities that she had always loved about him, and then a realization struck her. Why was he so different from everyone else? She saw some of the same qualities in Clyde and her father but not in many of the other people that she knew.

****

When Kimberly first approached Jordan about the affair, he denied it. Though she did not tell him how she knew, she pressed on with specific details and he finally admitted to it, apologized, and said he would end it. But it did not stop. Through the following weeks of listening to recorded conversations, Kimberly could tell that she was fighting a losing battle. She told Jordan last week that she wanted a divorce.

Within a day, Jake called her into his office for a private meeting.

"Look Kimberly, I've worked too hard and too long at setting up this election run and I can't afford to have any scandal come up, especially with needing a super majority to win."

"Why are you talking to me? It's Jordan, your DC Commander, that's responsible.”

“I’ve had a chat with him already and he’s promised to lay low.”

“Lay low? I don’t want him to lay low. I want no part of this and want a divorce from him.”

“You can have your divorce after the election. Until then, you’ll at least give the outward appearance that everything is normal.”

“And if I don’t?”

“I can make your life tough here. You’re already on my watch list for all of this environmental stuff that you’re working on that I haven’t approved. I can make it so that you’ll not be able to find work anywhere.”

“I’ll move to Percipience.”

“Ha! That’s never going to happen. Jordan has the right to see his kids. So you’ll stay in Epoch and you’ll cooperate. I’ll move you to a different division at the Re-Discovery Center so that you’re not working so closely with Allison, which should help. After the election, you can have your divorce, and I’ll find you a suitable job for a single mom with four children.”

Seeing no other choice, Kimberly agreed and left his office in tears.

That was only a week ago and Kimberly did not know if she could make it for three more months. She and Jordan no longer spoke to each other unless necessary, and their kids were noticing the tension as well.

There was not much she could do to keep her mind off of her broken marriage. Even though Jake had moved her to a different position at work, she still ran into Allison quite often. At home, there was Jordan; her only real escape was the church, which she attended regularly. For those few hours a week and the occasional counselling session with the pastor, she was thankful. The rest of the time she spent depressed and fearful of her future after the election.

****

Robert stood at the front of Elder's room, looking across the fifty men and women who were the leaders of the clan huts of Percipience. They usually met once a month to cover the general items needed to keep the village running, but Robert had called this special meeting and did not give them any advance warning as to what it was about.

"I think that over the last few hundred years, we have followed the guidelines and accomplished the goals outlined by Richard, our founder," Robert said. "We've worked through many issues and now have a lifestyle that's sustainable. However, this isn't enough. Our goal shouldn't be just to be sustainable but to make our world better. While we may feel that we have our house in order, we have neglected to look at our neighborhood, and this is where I have recently found an issue—one that I feel will change everything."

Not a sound could be heard in the room with everyone's eyes glued on Robert as he explained the potential runaway greenhouse gas problem and then went through the results of the research he had done. When he was finished, he looked across the room and noticed the hushed conversations going on amongst the crowd.

He continued, "I believe that we need to attack this on two fronts. The first is to figure out how, or maybe even where, we should live if the gasses get higher and the climate becomes more unpredictable. The second thing is working on a way to lower the gas levels."

A question came from the back of the room. "I can understand looking for a better area to live, but how can our little village do anything about a global problem like that?"

"I agree that it seems like far too big of a problem for our small village to do anything about, but that shouldn't stop us from trying. I've already spoken to Aaron and he has agreed to join our efforts. Before the Great

Loss, the world's population had the challenge of trying to reduce greenhouse gas levels while dealing with the economic growth machine that was responsible for generating more; it was nearly an impossible task. We don't have these issues. Instead, we just face the challenge of reducing the greenhouse gases that already exist. A monumental task, but also a completely different problem than what they faced."

Robert could see that the group was skeptical. "Back in the mid-twentieth century, it was discovered that CFCs caused a chain reaction that reduced ozone in our atmosphere, and it sure didn't take that much to make a big impact. What if we could develop something similar that would cause a chain reaction to reduce greenhouse gases? Perhaps we can develop something with this new nanotube technology that will scrub the atmosphere on a large scale. With our advanced research in biology, perhaps we can re-engineer plants to do something similar. There are many angles that we can approach this problem with."

Richard saw that the group was paying more attention now, but they still were not completely with him. "I believe that we can make a significant difference, and to that end, and from this day forward, we're going to have one additional goal for our villages. The goal is to focus on the reduction of greenhouse gases. It will be your job to ensure that this goal will be the focus of everyone at Percipience and Port Aspire."

"Are you certain this will happen?" came a question from the crowd. "This is a lot of effort for something that I don't think will impact us, at least not for a long time."

"Am I certain? No," Robert replied. "But I'm pretty sure, and there's a lot of evidence that says I'm right. But let me turn that question around. If I'm wrong, the worse that happens is that we waste some time with planning. If you're wrong and we do nothing, the consequences are pretty steep."

Robert was disappointed after leaving the meeting. He knew that the elders would do their best, but he could feel that their hearts were not in it.

7 STRESS

"Alright everyone, let's settle down," Lauren said to the group of her best students that comprised the Hive. They were gathered in a meadow close to Percipience. Lauren had brought Heather along as well, and she was currently concentrating on some butterflies that were circling her. "We've got a lot to go over today, so let's start with the event list for the Psychic Games that'll be held in about a month."

With an ever-increasing number of kids showing psychic abilities, the elders agreed to have the Hive become responsible for ensuring that there was no cheating at the spring and fall Games by monitoring that no one interfered with any events. Lauren had agreed to this but argued that the members of the Hive should still be allowed to compete but the elders did not want any part of it. They instead decided that to measure the strength of the psychic abilities for GDP purposes, a special annual Psychic Games would be introduced and they put Lauren in charge of it.

At first, Lauren did not think it would be too hard to organize, but as the number of entrants increased, she began to realize that there was a significant amount of work to be done. Events needed to be defined, schedules setup, and judges chosen along with food and entertainment for not only the contestants but the spectators as well, which was probably going to be the whole village.,

"I'm looking for ideas for events," Lauren said. "Let's start with events that are not directly competitive in nature—ones that test individual skills. My first idea is for a mind reading event. We could have twenty-five people scattered all over Percipience and the outlying area. Each participant would be shown a card with a different number and the test would involve determining where the person with a certain number is and how long it takes to detect. This would be good for an initial screening for the Hive. Any other ideas?"

"How about something that tests how many things can be controlled at once?" one ten-year-old suggested. "You could put a hundred balls on the ground, fifty black ones and fifty white ones, and then see who can lift the most of one color and they would be penalized if they also lifted the wrong color."

"That's good," Lauren said. "Any other suggestions?"

"Mommy, how about making butterflies form patterns?" came a suggestion from behind Lauren. The group turned their focus to Heather who had about twenty butterflies fluttering in front of her in a perfect figure eight.

"Oh, I like that," Lauren said. "Maybe not butterflies but something regarding controlling thoughts or actions of living things. Another good screen for the Hive as well."

"I've got one," a person in the front row said. "Let's have a contest where people guess what playing card you're going to pull from a shuffled deck before you pick it."

"Perfect," Lauren replied. "Testing out precognition abilities."

"What's the prize for winning?" came a question from the back of the group.

"That's a good question," Lauren replied. "I was thinking of maybe a trip on my husband's new airship to a destination picked by the winner."

"Nice!" said the child asking the question; several others showed excitement in both riding in the airship and going somewhere none of them had gone before. This started a firestorm of ideas on where they would like to go.

Lauren smiled as she saw the level of enthusiasm that they had. While they were talking about destinations, she started to think more about Heather's suggestion. It was a good one, but she needed something that would be more entertaining for the crowd. Something bigger than butterflies, something funny. She smiled as she thought of the perfect object for this contest.

A few days later, Lauren told Clyde about her plan. "No way!" he said. "Find some other mind to mess with!"

"It'll be harmless," Lauren said, "We'll get you some ear muffs so that you can't hear anything and a blind fold. You'll then be seated in a chair and each contestant will be challenged to get you to do or say something from a random selected card."

"What if they mess up? I may be walking around clucking like a chicken for the rest of my life."

Lauren giggled. "As appealing as that may be to me, it won't happen. But I anticipated your reluctance and have a special treat lined up for you if you agree." She looked around to make sure no one could overhear them and then decided to take no chances and leaned over and whispered into his ear.

Clyde's eyes grew wide. "Alec and Robert are good with this?"

Lauren nodded.

"I'm all in," Clyde said without hesitation. "Where are those ear muffs?"

****

The auditorium was at capacity when Robert entered for the Sunday morning service. He quickly spotted his wife who had saved him a place and sat down as the pastor was approaching the podium. The crowded service was usual for this non-denomination service. Though there were services for other faiths, such as Catholicism and Islam, this was by far the most popular. Whether the reason was for faith or simply community involvement, between all of the services, nearly the entire population of Percipience and Port Aspire attended church.

The pastor was an elderly woman who needed a staff to keep balance when walking. Her white hair and slightly hunched back gave no hint of her powerful voice and quick wit.

"Good morning," she said. "Today I'd like to talk a little bit about the Great Loss. All of you know the history behind it and the grave devastation that occurred during that time. The Great Loss doesn't just refer to the billions of people who died; it also refers to the loss of technology and knowledge. What did not get impacted though is our faith and beliefs, as this large congregation proves."

The pastor moved away from the podium and slowly waved her staff across the hall. "This is a non-denomination service, which means that amongst you, especially with a crowd of this size, we're going to have the entire spectrum of beliefs. From people who are certain there's a higher entity to people who are just as certain there isn't. There's representation of every major faith. However, what may come as a surprise to you is that every single one of you has had their faith compromised by the Great Loss.

"I've spoken before about the Golden Rule. It's throughout all of the major religions and is also the cornerstone to life for many who are certain that there is no God. The rule that I essentially thought was all about doing unto others as you'd have them do onto you. But despite countless hours going through the texts that pre-dated the Great Loss and far too many hours on the WISE system, I can't find the exception list for it that must exist."

Robert glanced around the room and it looked like most people were as confused about what was being said as he was. There were hushed whispers in the crowd and a general feeling of confusion. *Where's she going with this?*

"You see, before the Great Loss, if you ran into someone's car in a parking lot, you'd leave a note giving your information so they could contact you about repairs. You did this because of the Golden Rule and the thinking that if someone hit your car, you'd like them to do the same thing."

There was a general sense of agreement coming for the crowd.

"But there must have been an exception to this rule when dealing with future generations. Prior to the Great Loss, the pollution, resource usage, and economic problems were far greater than the generation at the time could handle. Yet, they seemed to have no problem with passing the issues over to future generations to deal with even though I am sure that they wouldn't want someone doing the same to them. It was not for a lack of knowledge either, they fully understood what they were doing, yet continued doing it even though there were simple things that could have been done to drastically reduce the impact to us, the future generation.

"Since this exception must have existed prior to the Great Loss, I am fearful that we may have lost other key points to our faiths. Maybe there was proof that we all evolved from clams."

This brought a chuckle from the crowd.

"Of course, your old pastor has not lost it, yet. I know that there wasn't an exception list to the Golden Rule and that the cause of the behavior before the Great Loss was that people's feeling of entitlement trumped the Golden Rule. This entitlement was similar to the Golden Rule in that it had no boundaries and went across all faiths and levels of believers.

With the crowd now fully engaged, the pastor went on to deliver the rest of her sermon on the topic of entitlement.

At the end of the service, Robert and his wife joined the line to exit the auditorium. They were close to the door when the pastor approached them and gave Robert a letter.

"What's this?" Robert asked.

"My bill," The pastor said without missing a beat. "Actually it's a letter addressed to you. It came up yesterday from Epoch with the supplies for their research staff. Even though our villages aren't officially communicating, there's been no objection to the churches throwing a bag aboard the supply plane once per month."

Robert thanked the pastor, returned to his wife, and left the auditorium. They were barely outside when Robert opened the envelope and read the contents within. He told his wife that he had some business to tend to and would meet her back at the clan hut shortly. He then went over to the town center and fired up the radio and was relieved when Alec answered.

"Alec, how soon can you finish your airship?"

"Pretty soon, maybe another month including test flights."

"Do you think you can make one of those test flights in two weeks? I just got a disturbing note and need some kind of transportation available exactly two weeks from today."

"Two weeks! That'll be tight, but if I cut a few corners and neglect your daughter and grandchildren, then I suppose I could do it."

"Good. Blame it all on me. I can't tell you the reason for the rush right now over the radio, but I will the next time that we meet face to face."

Robert then wrote a reply to the note, putting it in code so that only the intended party would know the real meaning of it. He then went over to the computer hut and put the note on the outgoing research note pile. *I hope it makes it and I hope that I'm not too late.*

.

****

Though she did not do it too often anymore, Kimberly still placed the recording device in her husband's office once in a while to see if by some miracle things had changed. The evening conversation that she had just listened to, however, confirmed that they had not and it brought tears again to her eyes.

She put away the recording device and got up to finish preparing supper. One of her children startled her as he came in the back door.

"Mom, I need you to send some money to school so that I can go on a field trip to one of the nearby deserted towns," he said as he handed her a permission form. "All of my friends are going. I have to go!"

Without really thinking about it, Kimberly signed the form, gave him the money, and then gave him a big hug. *I can't keep going like this. I need out of this relationship and I'm not leaving without my kids. But where can I go? Who can I turn to? Everything that I've tried over the last few months has failed. Jake knows everyone in Epoch, so I've no one here and he also won't let me go on resupply missions to Percipience anymore, cutting off that avenue too.*

Her thoughts evaporated and she tensed up as she heard the front door open, knowing that it was Jordan returning home from work.

He came into the kitchen. "Are you doing something behind my back?" he said accusingly, putting a piece of paper on the kitchen table. "This came in with the weekly research from Provenance."

Kimberly was facing the kitchen window and slowly turned around. "I'm not the one doing things behind people's back," she said as she picked up the paper. Her heart rate quickened as she saw it was a note directed to her from Robert.

"Jake has spoken to you numerous times and has forbidden it."

"But I…" she started to say but was interrupted by Jordan's rant.

"We're to put all of our resources into electronics and not into the emissions issue from the refinery. Also, I sure as heck don't want you having any communications with Robert or anyone else from Percipience."

Kimberly breathed a small sigh of relief as she picked up the paper. "I didn't initiate this. It's clear from this note if you even bothered to read through it."

Kimberly,

I hope that all is well with you and your family. Everything is going well here with the Fall Games and the new Psychic Games coming up soon. The only other new thing up here is that I've been in discussions with the other elders on the idea of building a stadium here.

I'm writing you to give you a heads up on the emissions work that we were working on before you left. At that time, we were concentrating on reducing emissions from the refinery near Epoch, but since then I've confirmed that the base atmospheric greenhouse gas level is much higher than we were assuming.

This will impact the calculations used in your emissions equations. The new constant that should be used in the equation is 09152232.0200.

Yours truly,
Robert

"Well, I've heard rumors that you're still working on it and that has to stop now!" Jordan said.

"What I do on my time is my business." Kimberly replied, "I certainly don't get involved in yours."

Kimberly stormed off to let the kids know that dinner was ready. As soon as she was out of view from Jordan, she let out a huge exhale and tried to calm down. Nearly at the breaking point, the news in the letter was the first glimmer of hope that she had let herself feel in months.

8 MAIDEN FLIGHT

From the time he walked off of the barge at Port Aspire, Robert could sense the difference. There was a buzz of activity, an intensity that was not at Percipience. There were construction sounds and people scurrying this way and that, including Clyde who was coming down to the dock carrying a large thin box.

"Hi chief. You've decided to slum it for a while, eh?"

"It's been about two years since I've been up here last. It's busy here."

"Today's pretty typical—lots to do. We want to get this place on the map and at the same time, save the world."

"Save the world?"

"Alec told us that we have a new goal: cleaning up the air. We're pretty tight on people, but we are giving it a shot. There's a group working on a mechanical device and I am working some biology angles."

"Do you know where I can find Alec?"

"Yes. Give me a sec," Clyde said as he put the box on a large fusion reactor that Percipience had shipped up on the barge. Robert watched as Clyde slung two narrow cables around the reactor and attached them to the box. He then pulled out a crank handle from his back pocket, inserted it into a small hole at the base of the box, and started to turn the crank. As he did so, the box started to grow higher and wider and was soon transformed into a large column about thirty feet in the air.

"There that should do it," Clyde said. As he took his hand off of the crated fusion reactor, it started to slowly lift up in the air. Clyde turned the crank to balance the crate so that it was floating at about chest height and then started to walk back up the dock towards Robert, pulling the reactor behind him with one hand.

"I've seen the samples of Alec's vacuum balloon, but this is incredible." Robert said.

"They're great and Alec has gone crazy with the idea. For instance, we're working on a design right now to see if we can replace our horizontal windmills with ones that are floating several thousand feet in the air where there's more wind and no birds to hurt. We're also trying to tie the same concept into cleaning the air. Anyhow, he's been working nearly day and night on his project for the last few months. The thing is huge and is up behind the main hemp field. Just start heading up that way. Trust me, you can't miss it."

Clyde was not kidding. As soon as Robert walked through the town and into the clearing of the hemp field, he could see the airship on a hill on the other side. From the distance, it looked complete and ready to go. As he approached the huge contraption, he noticed that it was hovering about six feet above the ground and he found Alec underneath it, finishing up painting the underside of the cabin a dull black color.

"My God, Alec; I knew that it was big, but this thing is enormous! How'd you built it so fast?"

"Well if we hadn't found that nanotube machine in the pyramid and I had to build it with normal materials, it would have taken a lot longer. Everything was so easy though with the nanotube material. Heck, I could pick up several of the three hundred foot rib supports by myself."

"Have you named it yet?"

"You're looking at the *Fly About Thing*. That's what Clyde started calling it, and it's kind of stuck."

"She's magnificent! Sorry to put a rush on you to finish it and not give you much time for test flights."

"Test flights? Who needs test flights?" Alec said. "Seriously though, the best we've been able to do is a couple of tethered tests. Tonight will be her first run."

"Alec, I have to say that I'm impressed. Building up the infrastructure for the new village, this magnificent craft, and as I heard from Clyde, working on cleaning the air—how in the heck do you motivate people to do all of this? At Percipience, I can't seem to get people moving on the new goal, at least not at this intensity."

Alec thought for a moment. "Not sure, really. Perhaps complacency has set in at Percipience. Things have been going smooth there for quite a while and people don't perceive that there's a real problem. I challenge the population here so much that they don't know what the word complacency even means."

Robert nodded while still looking at the airship. "Maybe that's the secret. Can you give me the tour of this thing? Oops, sorry, I mean the *Fly About Thing*."

"Well the large cube over at the end is the cargo container. There's also the cockpit and the cabin that are permanently attached. The cabin can hold about ten people and is equipped with a small galley and sitting and sleeping areas for longer trips."

"Impressive. You've done all of this in the last couple of months?"

"I had the cockpit and cabin pretty much done before we discovered the nanotube machine. Making the balloon and cargo containers from nanotube material was easy and fast. Here, let me pack up these painting supplies and then I'll show you inside."

Upon entering the cabin, Robert was impressed. There were several lounging chairs and tables bolted to the floor and full length windows on either side. The windows were angled so that the tops were farther out than the bottom so that people could lean over and look straight down. A hallway at the back of the cabin led to a small galley, washroom, sleeping area and a door at the back that led to the cargo area.

"The cargo bay has a large loading ramp at the back and the ability to detach if needed," Alec said. "But the really cool part is up here," he said pointing to a small spiral staircase that led up into the envelope section of the airship. Following Alec up the stairs, Robert had a bit of difficulty getting his broad frame through the opening in the ceiling. Once through, he was surrounded in darkness with the only light being provided from the opening he came through.

Alec flipped the light switch and the enormous area inside the envelope lit up. Robert eyes grew wide as he saw the network of catwalks, cables, and large tubes. All of the tubes were currently compressed like an accordion with twenty-five in the front of the room and an equal number at the back.

Alec pointed to one of the cylinders and hit a manual switch for a moment. The cylinder started to expand, pulled by several nanotube cables. "I can't show you it fully expanded since we'd start to get some lift even with a single tube expanded. Later during our flight, you should come back up here and see it all in full operation."

Robert was nearly beyond words. "This is amazing. The lift is caused just by the vacuum then? How high can it go?"

"I'm not sure but in theory with a fully loaded cargo bay it should be able to hit five thousand feet. After that the air starts to get too thin and I won't get as much lift."

Robert nodded in understanding and pointed to the two small cold fusion reactors. "Do you need both of these to power everything?"

"No. One can do the job, but I've tons of redundancy built in here to make it safe. If we're planning on going to Provenance in this someday, I don't want it to fail in the middle of the ocean."

Alec led Robert back down the staircase, headed to the front of the cabin, and opened the door to the cockpit. Robert could see that Alec had taken special care in building this area with varnished wood and polished metal on the dials and controls. There were two seats in the room and a lighted map table. What stood out though was the large wooden ship wheel at the front.

Alec noticed Robert eyeing the wheel. "Couldn't resist adding that in. We could've put in some sliders on the control panel for rudder control but I wanted to put this in instead." Alec's mood got a little more somber as he idly played with the wheel rotating it back and forth. "So about tonight— are you ready?"

Richard's smile disappeared as well. "Yes, we're ready. Like we discussed, ten men came up with me today to help out and they're waiting at the dock. They're the strongest and best skilled that Percipience has with various weapons; hopefully we'll not need them."

Alec nodded. "Alright, let's take this for its maiden voyage and then pick them up and go from there. I'd have liked to have had more time to test things out but our timetable doesn't allow it."

Alec went outside briefly to untie the tether cables and close the cabin ramp. He then returned to the cockpit. With Robert holding onto a hand rail, Alec reached for the controls and guided the airship quickly to a few hundred feet in the air. "Sorry about that," Alec said after noticing the look of discomfort on Robert's face at the sudden upward movement.

Alec adjusted the controls to gently engage the propulsion fans, and as the ship started to move forward, he spun the wheel to direct it towards Port Aspire's dock. Robert looked down through a window as they passed over the buildings of Port Aspire and saw people looking up at them and following them as the ship approached the ocean. With a couple of minor corrections, Alec brought the ship down so that it was hovering near the shore and a few feet above the water. He hit a switch to lower the main cargo ramp which should, if he calculated correctly, touch down on the sand of the beach.

"Robert, could you go back there and load up your men. I've things setup here to keep the ship stationary but I want to be here just in case they don't work."

Robert left to go to the back of the ship and returned after a short time. "Everyone is loaded up but we also picked up some riff raff."

"Hi Alec," Clyde said sticking his head through the cockpit doorway. "Robert told me about the little trip you two are going on. I thought I might as well join and cash in on Lauren's promise to me for helping out in her Psychic Games."

Alec looked to Robert. "You ok with this?"

"Sure. Clyde's stuff won't take very long."

Alec nodded and then looked towards Clyde. "Do you have your supplies ready?"

"You bet. I've been ready for over a week."

"Ok. Let's do it then," Alec said solemnly. "If we leave now, we'll get to Epoch right around our scheduled time of two in the morning." He then looked at Robert. "Last chance; you sure you want to do this?"

"No doubt at all. It may start another fight between our two villages, but I'll not stand by and let this happen."

"Ok then," Alec said as he closed the cargo ramp, guided the ship up to five hundred feet in the air, and then with the propellers engaged, turned the ship towards Epoch.

9 UNDER THE COVER OF DARKNESS

The sun had set several hours ago and the airship was about an hour away from Epoch. Alec flipped several switches on the console to turn off the running lights and told Robert to go and tell everyone that from here on in, to keep all lights off. Tonight was new moon and with the black exterior, no lights and electric propellers, the enormous ship was nearly undetectable.

Approaching Epoch at a high altitude, Alec drifted over the village until he was over the school's football stadium. After giving a warning to his passengers, he dropped the airship quickly unto the field and opened the rear cargo ramp. The ten armed men that Robert had taken with him immediately ran down the ramp and took up positions around the airship.

Clyde was heading down the ramp with a large roll on his shoulder and carrying a leftover paint canister that Alec had been using to paint the bottom of the airship. Robert ordered one of the armed men to go with Clyde to help him.

"Clyde, be quick, ok? We can't stay here very long," Robert said in an elevated whisper.

"Chill! This is going to take no more than fifteen or twenty minutes," Clyde replied and then he and his escort sprinted off towards the town center.

"This had better not mess up because of him," Alec said, and Robert nodded in agreement.

After a few minutes, Alec started to breathe a little easier. "Well, it looks like nobody noticed us landing."

"Yeah, but if anyone comes down one of those side streets, they'll spot us in a second. We can't be here for too long."

Fifteen minutes passed, then twenty. One of the guards spotted two figures coming across the field. With rifles at the ready, they waited until they could see who it was.

"Told you we'd be back in time," Clyde said. "Are we ready to go?"

"No, not yet," Robert said in a worried tone *Maybe we got our communications mixed up on the date, time, or place?*

His thoughts were interrupted by the guards who had detected more motion at the edge of the playing field. Within a minute, Robert recognized Kimberly and her four kids walking quickly towards them.

"Hurry," Robert said with relief. "We've been here long enough and need to leave."

As soon as everyone was back on the airship, Alec warmed them to hold onto their stomachs as he punched maximum lift and the airship shot up into the sky like a cannon ball. He stopped the ascent after three thousand feet, set course for Percipience, and then headed back to see how his passengers had managed through their departure.

"I thought I was in a spaceship for a minute there," Robert said. The cabin area was dim with only the small emergency lights on. "But it looks like everyone survived it. This is quite a ship you've built."

Kimberly came over. "I can't thank-you enough for taking the risk to get me and my kids."

"Don't mention it," Robert said. "From the message you got to me, I completely understand your need to get out of Epoch. You and your children have a new home in Percipience. I still can't quite believe Jordan and Allison's actions and how Jake has handled all of this. I would not have expected any of this."

"Me either," Alec said.

"For a moment there I was worried that you did not get or understand my response to the second note that you left me," Robert said.

"I was worried that you did not get my message in the first place," Kimberly said. "I was afraid it would get intercepted, but luckily no one looked through the church pouch. From your message back to me, it was easy to figure out the time and place."

"Dudes, can we turn on some lights now?" Clyde asked. "I want to use the next few hours to catch up on some reading."

"Sure, the lights are ok," Alec said. "We're far enough from Epoch now that they'll not be able to see us."

"How did your little mission go?" Robert asked Clyde.

"Perfectly. I wish I was around to see the end results, but hearing about them will be more than good enough. I even managed to add in a little added touch thanks to the paint I found in the back of the cabin."

"Do you have any extra books?" Alec asked.

"Yeah," Clyde said pointing to his backpack. "Help yourself. I grabbed a stack of them from the ones we brought over from Percipience."

Alec took a couple of books from Clyde's backpack. He casually flipped through one on electronics, decided it was too deep for casual reading, and then looked at the cover of the second book, *An introduction to Building Lasers*. He started to flip through it and did a double take. He closed the book and removed the paper cover and gasped.

"What's up?" Clyde asked.

Alec was furiously flipping through the pages of the book. "You're not going to believe this."

"What?" Robert asked, his interest now piqued.

"This is Richard's journal, as in Richard the founder of Percipience! He must've been hiding it in the elders' library all along!"

****

"Well this is a bloody mess!" Jake said to Jordan and Allison who were sitting on the other side of his desk.

"You can't find her or the kids?" Allison asked Jordan.

"No. I've called all of her friends and nothing."

"That's not our biggest problem," Jake said. "That damn banner that's flying over Epoch is." Jake was referring to a massive banner that was suspended so that it could be read from anywhere in Epoch: *A Vote for Jake Is a Vote to Legalize Marijuana.* "Why isn't that thing down yet? People are going to see it and think that I am in favor of it."

"We've tried sir," Jordan replied. "We don't know what's holding it up in the air and it seems to be bullet proof as well. Who put it up there? Was it one of your opponents?"

"No. I am pretty sure it is the same group that's responsible for kidnapping your family," Jake said as he took a piece of paper out of his pocket and slid it across the desk. "This is one of my election posters that I found downtown early this morning. There are several more marked up the same way."

Jordan unfolded the piece of paper. There was a large picture of Jake and his slogan with some of the letters modified. What used to read "Vote for Jake, Lower Taxes! Power for the People!" had been changed to read "Vote for Jake, Flower Power for the People!" along with crudely drawn longer hair on Jake's picture.

60

Jake noticed Jordan trying to suppress a laugh. "There's only one person I know of that would do this and that's Clyde! I'm guessing that it was him and perhaps some more from Percipience must have been here last night, picked up your family, put up that blasted banner, and took off back to Percipience. I've made a call to the computer team up there to confirm. We should know pretty soon."

"I wonder how they got here," Jordan said.

"That doesn't matter," Jake said. "What matters is getting that banner down and keeping Kimberly's disappearance under wraps until after the election. I want you two to stay away from each other until then. Jordan, that banner must be anchored somehow to the ground; put every person on finding it and if anyone asks about your family, tell them that they decided to make a trip to Percipience for a vacation."

Jordan nodded in agreement. *I'm sure that Alec had a big part in this, too. He is probably laughing his head off right now on how he pulled a fast one on me. Well we'll see who gets the last laugh.*

****

"It works like a dream," Robert said to Aaron over the radio. "Incredible lift and the person that designed and built it has put in several fail safes."

"I'd very much like to see this airship of yours," Aaron said. "Something like that would be very useful over here. We have built up the nanotube machine as well but are using its products mostly for standard construction and nothing like this. It gets its lift through using a vacuum, huh?"

"Yes, it is kind of hard to explain. I've been talking to the other elders over here and we agree that since we now have this airship, it is high time that we make a trip over to see you."

Aaron agreed enthusiastically, and the two men laid out a plan for a trip within the next month.

After the conversation was over, Aaron had his assistant flick the switch on the radio. *Well, it looks like the friendship that Robert and I've developed over the last several decades is about to be put to the test.*

Robert flicked the switch to turn his radio off. *Well we'll finally see what other things Aaron has been hiding from me.*

10 VICTORY

Epoch Times – October 1, 2032

Well, he needed a super majority to win it all and that is exactly what the former city manager got. Receiving nearly ninety percent of the vote, "Flower Power" Jake as he's become known by was very humble during his acceptance speech at his campaign headquarters after the polls had closed. The exit polls are contributing to the sudden policy change a few weeks ago to push for the legalization of marijuana to the surge in his popularity.

****

Jordan didn't even raise his head from his desk as he heard the door to his office open.

"Good Afternoon!" Jake said as he came in and sat down in a chair. "Still feeling a bit tired, huh?"

"How in God's name can you be so full of energy?" Jordan said, finally lifting his head to look at Jake. After the election results came in the previous evening, he, Allison, Jake and several people from the campaign team went out on the town and did not finish until nearly sunrise.

Jake ignored Jordan's question. "I see that someone finally got that damn banner down."

"Yeah, I got the details this morning. With the rain yesterday, someone finally spotted one of the guide wires as it had water running down it. Extremely thin material too. Anyhow, once they found one, the other was easy to find and they pulled it down. What was strange about the whole thing is that they didn't think it was a balloon after all that was supporting it because when they punctured it, air went into it instead of out."

Jake shrugged his shoulders. "Whatever. I'm going to have to thank Clyde though for getting me elected. Without the banner and my new nickname, it would've been very close."

"But now you need to follow through and get pot legalized."

"I've thought about that. Though I'm not in favor of it, I'll set it up so that only the town can sell it legally and then put a big tax on it. Anyhow, I need to get going. I have to get to the television studio for an interview to tell people what they should be concerned about. I just stopped by to find out about the banner."

After Jake left, Jordan had a long nap in his chair and then started to do one final review of a map of the area surrounding Percipience when Allison came in with a big smile on her face. She walked behind his desk, put her arms around him, and gave him a soft kiss on the neck. "Well, now that this darn election is over and Jake has won, we shouldn't have to keep us a secret anymore, right?"

Jordan barely seemed to notice or respond.

"What's eating you?" Allison asked.

"Sorry, hun," Jordan said, reaching back to stroke her arm. "Just thinking about this plan we have against Percipience. Things have changed since Kimberly and the kids are up there now. It's my kids that I'm really worried about."

Allison gave him an affection hug. "We talked about this last week. There'll be enough warning. They'll be safe."

"I hope so. Well, let's get going, it'll be dark soon."

Flying through the night sky, the small plane headed north, taking care to take a wide berth around the Percipience area and the Hive protection grid.

Jordan was at the controls and Allison sat beside him in the copilot's seat, occasionally running her hand affectionately through his hair or rubbing his arm.

With a smile Jordan turned to her. "Nearly there. We'll be landing pretty soon."

The plane touched down on a lake and Jordan and Allison put on their heavy backpacks.

"The site is a couple of miles in from here," Jordan said.

"Well, you just be darn careful. With what's in your backpack, one slip could spell disaster."

With heavy cloud cover and nearly a new moon, the night was particularly dark and Jordan appreciated the night vision goggles that Allison had brought along. Being extra careful, the trip took longer than expected, but eventually they arrived at a worn down fence from before the Great Loss. Someone recently had propped up a battered sign next to the fence.

Restricted Area, No Trespassing
Use of Deadly Force Authorized

The fence did little to slow them down, and soon they were looking at what remained of a military weapons storage facility that had been buried into a hillside. Sometime during the last few hundred years a creek had diverted towards it, wearing down the hill and one of the walls of the facility, exposing the inner storage area. Being late fall, the creek level was low making it easy for Jordan and Allison to cross it and enter the room, which was dry.

Jordan pointed out the water level marks that were on the remaining walls. "During spring, this room must get really flooded."

"Are those the missiles?" Allison asked, pointing to six large rectangular cement slabs.

"They must be. The cement casings are the work of Robert around ten years ago. He developed cement that acted as a radiation shield and entombed these leftover nuclear missiles that had started to leak."

Allison put down her pack and pulled out a cordless electric drill. "Well, let's get to work."

"Aye, captain." Jordan said as he delicately put down his pack that contained the **hydrofluoric acid that Allison had made over the last six months.** He took the drill and started to drill a series of small holes with a slight downward angle along a side corner of one of the cement boxes. While he was doing this, Allison took out hoses and containers from her pack and started to assemble them together.

When Jordan was done, he took the hose assembly and set it up on the cement box, putting a hose into each of the freshly drilled holes. The other end of the hoses merged together at a central container that was on a stand on the cement box.

"Are you sure this is going to work?" Jordan asked.

"Yes, of course. Though this is an extremely corrosive acid, the hoses and container are made from a material that will not be effected by it. We'll fill up the container with the acid and then control the flow to the hoses with these valves. The container holds about three gallons; I've tested it out and it'll last about two weeks before running out."

Jordan nodded. "A slow continuous flow of acid into these holes should weaken the cement and then when we set off a small explosive, the cement box should crack open and it'll look like a natural failure caused by the heat built up inside the container."

"All seems like a lot of work. Are you sure we just can't blow it up now with a big explosive?"

"If we did, Robert would blame Epoch for sure, and who knows what kind of retaliation he would do. The man is out of control given what he did to Epoch ten years ago. No, this has to look like a natural failure resulting in more air contamination than when Robert fixed it last time."

They carefully filled the container with the acid and Allison set the valves to control the flow. After a few minutes, a sizzling sound could be heard coming from the holes. Satisfied that everything was working, they headed back to the plane to return to Epoch before sunrise.

****

The ball darted this way and that on the empty playing field to the cheers from the large crowd that were sitting on a hillside watching the event. Lauren had her doubts when the suggestion came up for psychic soccer as an event for the games, but now she could see that it was the most popular event both with the spectators and the players.

Each team had five players and they had to work together to try and control the ball while fending off attacks from the opposing team that were targeted at getting them to lose their concentration.

The ball stopped at midfield, moving only a few feet in each direction as the teams struggled to get control. Suddenly, the ball went straight up about ten feet and with great velocity shot across the field and through the goal followed by high fives and hugs by the team that scored the goal.

The individual events went smoothly with the most popular one being the thought control contest. Clyde was a natural for the test subject and had the crowd in tears of laughter with his antics. Though several contestants were able to get him to recite phrases and go through physical motions, whenever Clyde had control of himself, he would recite silly limericks or perform funny actions like pretending he was a monkey.

There was little doubt that with her level of skill, in a few years Heather would be the clear winner of the overall competition. She was easily beat out this year by her brother Logan, who had benefitted from several more years of practicing to hone his skills and practice multi-tasking.

For his prize, Logan choose to have an airship ride north to a town called Drumheller that, before the Great Loss, had a massive dinosaur fossil collection in several museums. Logan reasoned that even if the museums had deteriorated, there should still be lots to see, and he was right. A dozen kids made the first trip and it was such fun that Lauren opened the trip up to all of the kids, psychic or not. The response was so overwhelming that Alec and Clyde had to design a new cargo container that would seat about one hundred people. Even with this new cargo bay, Alec had to make several trips to accommodate the demand.

11 CONTACT

Alec had his arm around Lauren as they gazed through the window at the ocean as the *Fly About Thing* glided a few hundred feet above the water. In the distance, they could see the retreating Hawaiian island of Lanai, which they had used as a stopover on their trip to Provenance. In addition to Alec and Lauren, Robert had also picked himself, Clyde, Heather, and Kimberly to join in the journey.

"I'm going to get another piece of pineapple from the galley," Lauren said. "Did you want some?"

"You've got to be kidding," Alec replied. "Didn't you get your fill yesterday? I think each of us must have eaten at least two."

"But they're so good! After this trip, we're going to have to make a regular run out here every few months to get some more."

"Hmm. I like that idea; maybe just the two of us will go," Alec said while hugging her a bit closer.

Lauren glowed inside as she snuggled up closer to him. *I can't imagine a life any better than this. I am so lucky and grateful for having Alec a part of my life. I can't even begin to fathom how Kimberly is feeling after what happened with Jordan.*

Robert had asked Kimberly to come along to get her mind off of the last few horrible months that she had been through. Though she initially wanted to take her children as well, Robert convinced her that they would be fine under the care of the others of his clan hut. Even after just the first week of the journey, he could see that she was doing much better as she started to show excitement over his plans for a new device to reduce greenhouse gases.

Clyde spent his time during the journey engrossed in reading Richard's journal. Once in a while he would call out "Aha!" as a revelation hit him as to why things were the way they were. Heather spent a great deal of her time sitting in a chair and looking in the direction of the window, but she was more in a trance than enjoying the scenery.

Alec sat down beside her after he noticed a prolonged look of concentration on her face. "Where's my little girl?"

There was no response for a minute and then Heather looked at him. "Jeremy's dad wants to talk to you."

Lauren turned around, "What?"

Everyone stopped what they were doing and stared at the five-year-old.

"He wants to know where we are. Jeremy told him we're flying over water and he doesn't understand."

Heather had never mentioned anything about her imaginary friend having parents but Alec played along, got up, and went and got a world map from the cockpit. "We're right about here." He pointed to a location south of the Hawaiian Islands. "Where's Jeremy's father?"

Her answer made everyone who was listening to the conversation stare even harder. "Mars," she said then looked at the map in front of her. "Daddy, where is Mars? Jeremy keeps saying the dirt is red and I don't see anything red on this."

Lauren, Alec, and Clyde looked at each other. "Could it be?" Lauren asked no one in particular. "We know there was reference to a Mars colony in Richard's journal but also that they'd lost communications with them twenty years after the Great Loss."

"Man, could they have survived this long? Why haven't we heard from them?" Clyde said.

"Well, for starters, we haven't been listening," Alec said. "For Mars, we'd need to setup a tracking dish antenna. The original Percipience residents took it down after waiting years with no word from Mars and stored it in the warehouse."

Alec turned to Heather. "Can you ask Jeremy to ask his dad how long they've been on Mars?"

After a brief pause, she said, "His dad said two hundred years and then something about Pleasant Belief. Where is Mars, Daddy? It must be big because Jeremy said there are thousands there."

Robert got up slowly and shook his head. "There's no way she could have known that. This must be the real deal. Can you imagine? A whole colony, at least the size of Percipience, on a different planet?"

"Mars is a planet far away from us," Alec told his daughter. "Tell Jeremy that we live on Earth. Can you ask him if they can use a radio to talk to us?"

"He said that his dad said yes and that he's acting kind of crazy and is laughing and jumping up and down."

"Robert, you're the boss," Alec said. "We're about two days from Provenance. Do you want to turn around and go back to try and setup the radio or continue on?"

"Full speed to Provenance. They're not as big or as advanced as us so I doubt they'll have the equipment needed, but they might. If they don't, then we'll cut our trip there short and head back to Percipience."

"Ok, sounds like a plan," Alec said and then turned back to Heather. "Tell Jeremy that we're far away from our radio right now and that you'll let him know when we are ready, probably in a couple of weeks from now."

"Jeremy said ok and something about his dad needed some time, too."

Robert looked over towards Alec. "Can you make this *Fly About Thing* go any faster?"

"I think I may be able to do that," Alec replied with a wink and headed to the cockpit.

****

Jeremy's dad, Conner, was jubilant. "I have to admit, I've always wondered if your friend Heather was real or not. I don't have a clue how this ability of yours works, but this confirms that it's for real. Great idea on asking her to ask her dad."

"Yeah, I should've thought of that earlier," Jeremy said. "She's too young to understand about planets and the solar system."

"It's hard to imagine. We'll soon have the first radio communications with Earth in over one hundred and fifty years."

After the Great Loss, communication was kept up with Percipience for about twenty years, but then there was a hardware failure on the radio transmitter on Mars. With the struggle of surviving taking precedence over everything else, attempts to fix the radio were not done for over a decade, long after Percipience had given up listening.

"The first thing we need to establish is their level of technology," Conner said. "Heather said they were flying over the ocean, so they're not in the Dark Ages. But, do they have the capability of spaceflight? That is the big question. We can only hope that they do and that they can get to us quickly."

12 PROVENANCE

A day ahead of schedule, the *Fly About Thing* approached the coastline of Australia.

"How far are we away from Provenance?" Lauren asked.

"That depends on how good I've been at navigating," Alec replied. "If we're where I think we are, then Provenance should be only a few hours down this coastline."

Everyone on the airship was peering out the windows, looking ahead to get the first glimpse of the village but were startled when two planes approached from the rear of the airship and quickly flew past on either side.

"Where in the heck did they come from?" Alec said as he flicked a switch to turn on the radio.

"Aaron never mentioned anything about planes!" Robert said.

The planes did two more passes before Alec found the radio frequency that they were on.

"Unidentified airship, you are in restricted airspace. Please identify yourself. Failure to do so will result in us taking defensive measures; we have authorization to shoot you down. This is your final warning."

Alec clicked on the transmit button. "This is the airship *Fly About Thing* from Percipience. We have Robert on board who has an invitation from Aaron to meet him in Provenance. We're unarmed."

There was an eerie pause in the communication. The radio then crackled to life with a friendlier tone. "Roger, *Fly about Thing*. We have confirmed your information. You're about one hundred miles out from Provenance on your current heading. We'll provide an escort for you to the airport, which is east of the town."

Alec looked at Robert with wide eyes and a questioning shrug of his shoulders.

"I guess we need to do what they say. We're going to have to be cautious though. I'll go back and tell the others to keep their eyes open and lips sealed. Aaron knows a great deal about us, but there's no need to tell him more until we know what's going on."

"How about Heather's friend Jeremy and Mars?"

"We're especially going to keep that bit of information to ourselves," Robert said as he headed back to the main cabin.

Alec paused for a moment and then flicked the transmit switch. "Roger that. Proceeding directly to Provenance's airport and we appreciate the escort."

"Roger. By the way, nice anagram name for your airship."
Alec sighed and called back to Robert who was leaving the cockpit. "Tell Clyde that I want to know what the ship's anagram means!"

As they moved down coastline, it did not take long before the travelers started to see signs of civilization. However, unlike Percipience where living and work structures were not visible until you were right over top of them, Alec could see large buildings grouped together. It was immediately obvious that Provenance was much larger than Aaron made it sound to be.

From their aerial view, the airport and its several landing strips were easily spotted. Alec guided the airship towards it. As they approached, Alec could make out a group of people, most in a formation. Deciding that this was their reception party, he set the airship as close to them as he dared.

Alec and Robert were the first to disembark and were soon joined by the rest of the group as they were greeted by music performed by a military band and a platoon standing at attention. In front of the platoon were a couple of armed security personnel flanking a man wearing a high-ranking insignia on his uniform and an older woman wearing a colorful abaya.

Robert was about to step towards the man when the woman stepped forward and raised her hand to shake his. "Hi. You must be Robert. Welcome to Provenance." Her voice was pitched slightly lower than a normal woman's voice.

Robert raised his hand to shake hers while he examined her in detail. She was definitely older than him as could be seen from the white streaks in her dark hair and the age lines on her face. Her skin tone was darker and her deep blue eyes reminded him of Heather's. All of a sudden he had a revelation causing him to smile. "Hi Erin. Yes, I'm Robert. This may sound strange but in all of the years that we have spoken over the radio, I thought you were Aaron, a man!"

Erin laughed. "That's funny. But it's happened several times before. There's a small cyst on my vocal chords that I guess makes me sound a bit like a man. I on the other hand, had no idea that I was speaking with a giant. My hand looks like a child's when compared to yours."

"You're not the only surprise either," Robert said. "Provenance is much bigger than you had me believe."

"Sorry about the deception," Erin said. "We do this for security in case there are others out there who may take us for a threat. It is a policy that my military commander insists upon." She pointed to the man beside her.

"Well, you sure surprised us, that's for sure," Robert said and then started the introductions, beginning with Lauren.

"Ah, so you're the queen of this Hive protection system that I've heard so much of," Erin said.

"I guess that's one way to put it," Lauren replied.

"Well, you can take a holiday while you're here. We're your allies." Erin then looked down at Heather and immediately noticed the piercing light blue eyes. "You must be Heather. I think our eye color is nearly the same."

Heather did not reply as she moved closer to her mom.

Erin gave out a raspy laugh. "Shy, eh?" She then looked at Alec. "I'm going to take a guess that you're Alec and the creator of this magnificent ship. We have a good sized air fleet but nothing like this in it, and I can already see many uses for it. Would you mind giving a tour to my engineers later today? They've been most curious ever since Robert told us about it."

"Sure. I can do that. How big is Provenance?"

"Around forty-five thousand now if you include the satellite villages," Erin replied and then finished up the introductions by shaking Clyde's and Kimberly's hands. The general stepped forward and suggested that they head to a set of vehicles waiting nearby.

"You arrived a day ahead of when we were expecting you," Erin said. "You'll have to forgive me as I tend to some other business this afternoon, but my General will take you for a tour of our city and then I'll catch up with all of you for the evening meal."

Erin departed with her entourage of guards while everyone else boarded a waiting bus.

"All of this is powered by oil, I assume?" Alec asked the general as they left the airstrip, pointing to the airplanes and vehicles.

"Yes. We were fortunate in that area," he replied. "After the Great Loss, this village was much like yours; however, a few years after that a large group of people arrived from the Middle East. They said that they were part of a group called CURE. They initially had gone to the European village site but it had been gutted prior to the loss, so they decided to make their way here. This group had extensive knowledge of the drilling and refinement of oil and we had a refinery online before the oil supplies ran out. Before your help in finding the cold fusion reactor, oil was the best source of portable power that we had. We're slowly converting over from oil, but once an infrastructure is in place, it takes a while to change over."

"But doesn't that kind of go against everything that our villages were set up for to begin with?" Robert asked.

"Yes and no. CURE does have some of the same goals that the Pleasant Belief foundation had but with some key differences. The initial rules set down for the villages, the ones you live by, are far too restrictive. We believe that the planet can easily sustain billions of people like before the Great Loss with a few basic rules."

"Such as?" Alec asked.

"No livestock—pretty much a vegetarian-based society. No fertilizers, insecticides, and the like. Far higher concentration of public transit and tighter emission laws. With these few rules, many of the problems that were around before the Great Loss would have gone away."

They were driving past several large structures that Alec asked about.

"Those are apartment structures. The only single dwelling homes here belong to the rich. Everyone else are in these complexes. The higher population density is cheaper to setup and takes far less resources. Overall, I think you'll find that we're a nice blend between your way of living and the world before the Great Loss. We have kept some of the initial rules, such as no elected officials, but due to our bigger size we needed to put in a currency to allow for people to trade goods and services."

"Weapons and military as well," Clyde said pointing to the soldiers that were in the back of the bus.

"Yes, and thankfully as well. During the first few decades after the Great Loss, there were several raiding parties that tried to steal things. I think it was because Australia is isolated from the other continents resulting in a higher percentage of survivors from the virus."

"Another thing that we did not continue with here is the GDP," continued the general who then pointed to Robert. "Though by looking at the size of you, I wish we had. If all our soldiers were your size, we'd be unstoppable."

The rest of the afternoon was spent touring factories, stores, and greenhouses.

The general explained a bit more to the group. "Except for the hardiest of plants, everything is grown indoors now with hydroponics. The weather is too unpredictable. We seem to get a major storm through here at least once every few months."

The downtown was much larger than Epoch's, and Alec thought of Allison and how much fun she would have shopping in all of the stores. The bus finally pulled up to a large and impressive single dwelling house.

"This is a combination of Erin's home and the central command center for both the military and Provenance as a whole."

As they disembarked from the bus, they were greeted by Erin from the front landing. Dismissing her guards and the general, she took them for a personal tour of her home and command center before leading them to the dining hall, which had an elaborate feast laid out. They sat down for the evening meal that consisted entirely of vegetarian items. Lauren was about to serve herself some stew, which smelled appealing, when she noticed that the rest of the large table had not started yet.

"We're in the practice of saying grace here prior to our meals," Erin said, and everyone bowed their heads while she gave thanks for their meal.

"Is religion a big factor here?" Alec asked as he remembered being forced to attend services when he grew up in Epoch.

"I wish it was," Erin replied. "Initially yes, but as the years have passed, church attendance across all denominations is down, especially with the younger population."

"We don't have that problem at Percipience," Robert said, "If anything it's the opposite and there's a constant challenge to schedule our auditorium for religious functions. Especially for the non-denomination functions."

"Epoch has the same problem as here with declining attendance," Alec said.

"Well, that makes sense," Clyde said casually as he took another large forkful of stew and then realized that the conversation had stopped and everyone was looking at him.

He gulped down the mouthful of stew. "Well, it's obvious, isn't it? Most religions are based on faith and belief—that there's more than our physical world and us on it. To follow something like that, you must submit yourself to it and realize that you're a small part of something much bigger. Even with religions that don't believe in a creation God, there's usually an expectation of showing gratitude and humility."

"So?" Alec said

Clyde looked around the table and realized that he was the center of attention. "Well, at Epoch and Provenance, the culture tends to promote entitlement. This makes people more self-centered, especially the youth as the sense of entitlement grows. As people get a greater sense of self-importance, they feel less of a need to become part of something bigger and less of a need to show gratitude for things they receive."

"And at Percipience they don't?" Robert asked.

"No, of course not. With no currency, personal possessions, or special privileges, individualism does not have a chance to start. Look at yourself for example. Even though you're the leader of the village, you still take your turn in weeding the gardens and you sleep on a mat in your clan hut with everyone else."

"You need to smoke more of your plants. You're wrong on this one," Alec said. "It's more to do with science and the conflicts there with rationalizing it with books like the Bible and the Quran. As the younger population understands more science, the rationalization becomes harder and harder."

"No way, man. People in Percipience have just as strong of a science background as those in Epoch and I assume as Provenance as well," Clyde said while lining up another forkful of stew. "Science can neither prove nor disprove God because it's a belief. People use it though as a good excuse to not participate in any religion, even the ones without a creation God."

The group debated on the topic throughout the rest of the meal. After dinner was finished, Lauren, Kimberly, and Clyde left to return to the airship to put Heather to sleep, leaving Erin, the general, Robert, and Alec at the dinner table.

'So, there was more to my invitation than to just meet you," Erin said. "We could have flown over to see you at any time over the last few decades but choose not to take a chance and disclose our size or abilities."

"To whom?" Robert asked.

"Epoch or perhaps a city that we haven't heard of yet."

"I don't see Epoch as being much of a threat to you. Not with your size and military," Alec said.

"Maybe. The sterility trick that Robert pulled off was ingenious, and we thought that would keep them under control for quite a while, but now they seem to be growing faster than ever. They've even formed an alliance with several villages. Combine this with their consumption-based attitude similar to what existed before the Great Loss and they're a real threat."

"So what are your plans?" Robert asked.

"We'll take control of Epoch and the Alliance very soon. That's the real reason that I wanted you here, to make sure that my assumptions are correct and to gather extra intelligence that may be useful."

She obviously does not know that I'm from Epoch and still have family there! Alec thought.

Erin saw the look of concern on both Robert and Alec's faces. "Your villages don't have to worry about an attack from us. We both have the same basic principles. Your limited size and slow growth rate pose no threat at all to us."

"What do you mean by 'take over'?" Alec asked.

"We'll apply whatever force is necessary until we have control over the government, military, and people. I don't think that there will be too many casualties since we plan on intimidating them with sheer numbers right from the start. This is one of the questions that I wanted to ask both of you. The leader of Epoch—from the radio transmission we have intercepted, I think his name is Jake. What kind of character does he have? If shown right away that he doesn't stand a chance, do you think he'll make the right decision and surrender or will he fight to the end?"

Robert and Alec exchanged looks and then Alec gestured for Robert to speak. "I think Jake is a proud and intelligent man. If shown that he doesn't have a chance, my guess is that he'd surrender and then try to get himself a place of power within the new regime."

"Precisely what I thought too," Erin said looking pleased.

"When do you plan on doing this?"

Erin smiled but would not give them more details other than "very soon" despite Alec pressing for more.

After spending a little while longer talking to Erin, both Alec and Robert got up and said it was time to call it a night. They walked back to the airstrip for quite a while in silence before Alec spoke. "Well, I sure wasn't expecting any of this."

"Me neither."

"We need to leave here soon. I need to warn my parents over in Epoch. Do you think CURE's way is better than what we have at Percipience?"

"Well, it's better than Epoch's approach or to that prior to the Great Loss but it'll still run into problems," Robert replied. "It works now since they're able to expand rapidly with no restrictions on resources, but introducing currency to support specialization of labor will mess things up. Remember what we read from Richard's diary. 'Economics trumps everything else.' When they need to start making real decisions and sacrifices because resource are getting tight, that's when they'll go the same path as before the Great Loss, guaranteed."

"Yeah, that's exactly what I was thinking too. What do you think our next steps should be?"

"I don't trust them. I think we'll tell them that we've got some emergency in Percipience that we need to deal with and get out of here as fast as we can within the next few days. After that, I'm not sure."

13 SURREPTITIOUS OPERATIONS

The sun was rising as Jordan returned to Epoch from a flight out to the old army base that he and Allison had visited two months ago. Though they had made a couple of trips up to the site since to refill the acid tank, he made this last trip on his own to minimize any chance of Hive detection. With the purpose of this trip being to remove all evidence that the site had been visited recently and to set a small explosive thermite charge to go off in two days, this trip had the highest probability that the Hive would detect a threat, so the fewer people thinking about it the better.

He entered his office in the DC and was shocked to find Jake sitting in his chair mulling over some papers that were on his desk.

Jake looked up. "Jordan, are you planning things behind my back?"

Jordan's mouth went dry as his mind raced. *How did he find out?* "What are you referring to?"

"That's not a clear answer," Jake said as he focused his gaze and paused for a moment.

"No, I'm not hiding anything," Jordan said as he glanced at his desktop and wondered if there was any incriminating evidence there in plain sight. "I was just curious as to what you're referring to."

"There was a report that came in last night from one of the leaders down south that there were sightings of large troop movements being spotted there. Do you know something that I don't?"

Jordan tried not to show the feeling of relief that flooded through him. "No, I don't know anything at all about it, but I'll look into it and get back to you."

Jake got up from Jordan's chair and gave the young man one more prolonged gaze. "You do that, son." He patted him on the back and walked out of the office.

After Jake left, Jordan exhaled deeply. *What's he doing here so early in the morning? There's something else on his mind other than these sightings of troop movements. Does he know something about what Allison and I are up to?*

****

With all of the internal and external lights off, the *Fly About Thing* drifted undetected once more high in the night sky over Epoch. Though Robert wanted to get back home as soon as possible, he agreed to let Alec stop at Percipience first to warn them about the upcoming raid by Provenance.

"Hang on, we're going down," Alec said, guiding the airship down quickly to the same location in the football stadium that he had landed on before.

Leaving Robert at the controls of the airship, Alec headed towards his parent's home. It took a minute of continuous doorbell ringing before the outside light came on and the door opened.

"Alec! What are you doing here at this time of night?" Jake said.

"Dad, I don't have much time but I've come to warn you about an imminent attack on Epoch and the rest of the Alliance."

"Attack? Who would be stupid enough to attack us? It's not Robert is it?"

"No, it's not Percipience," Alec said shaking his head, "It's Provenance—a village in Australia that was setup at the same time that Percipience was."

"I've heard of it. From what we have picked up on the radio, it's smaller than Percipience so it couldn't pose a threat to us."

"We've been there and all of the communications that they publicly broadcast are a decoy. The place is huge and they have a large military."

"How did you get there? When is this attack?"

84

"Long story, but I built an airship. As for when, I don't know exactly, but it'll be soon."

Jake thought back to the previous morning and the report of troop movements to the south. "I'll talk to Jordan in the morning and we'll take appropriate action."

"Good, because I doubt if he'd listen to me," Alec said. There was a pause. "How are things going for you, Dad?"

"I'm doing fine, son, though I do miss you. You're doing fine? Lauren and your family doing ok?"

"Yes, everything is well. We need to somehow break this barrier between you and Robert and get our villages talking again."

"I'd like that very much," Jake said. "But I don't see that happening anytime soon, and I fear that it would end up in confrontation again anyhow."

"You're probably right. Anyhow, I must go. Tell Mom to be safe over the next few days and that I love her." Alec slipped back into the darkness to return to the airship.

****

"And you believe him?" Jordan said to Jake the following morning after he recounted the late night visit by Alec.

"I see no reason for him to lie to me."

"Robert probably put him up to it. I don't trust either of them, especially since it was probably them that kidnapped Kimberly and the rest of my family. Why don't you let me take care of this problem once and for all? We could take them out within a day with the military advantage that we have."

"No! We're not going to do that. I think his story is legit and it also lines up with the report of large troop movements to the south. I want you to send all of the extra men and equipment we have down there over the next few days."

"Well, I think it is a waste of time, but I'll get moving on it," Jordan said. *What kind of game is Alec up to now? Well, after tonight, it won't matter anyway.*

14 DESCTRUCTION

Throughout Percipience, the nighttime sounds of the forest were interrupted by hundreds of soft beeps. Alec awoke to the small chirps and immediately realized that it was the personal radiation monitors. It only took him a second longer to figure out that there must be some kind of wide spread radiation going through the village. Alec's first thought was a memory of his friends down in the Smokey mountain range over a decade ago. It only took two weeks for their whole town to be wiped out by some kind of radiation cloud.

Alec woke up Robert from a deep slumber and brought him up to speed with the situation at hand. Robert reacted quickly, sending people to alert the other clan huts. Lauren went to the lab to get a better quality radiation monitor. He then sent another person to radio over to Port Aspire to see if they were also impacted.

"Where's it coming from?" Robert asked to no one in particular.

"I've been wondering that too," Alec said. "We need to figure that out in order to avoid it. That is if we can."

Lauren returned from the lab and there was a small measure of relief as they discovered that the radiation levels were not too high.

"With these levels, people will be impacted after about a day's exposure. Two days of exposure would start to be lethal, at least for the elderly and very young." Robert said.

One of the men came running into the clan hut. "Port Aspire says that they're not detecting anything," he said while catching his breath.

"OK, so they're upwind from us. That's good news," Robert said. "Until we understand better what's going on, we're going to pack up essentials from here and move everyone there. Alec, I want you to transport the elderly and children in your airship. Everyone else walks.”

It was late in the afternoon by the time Alec had returned to Percipience from his third round trip to Port Aspire. By this time, Percipience was pretty much vacated with an overloaded barge pulling out from the dock and the rest of the residents having left to walk on foot to Port Aspire.

Robert helped him load the last of the critical equipment onto the airship and then returned from the Research Lab with two radiation suits.

“I’ve been thinking about this all day and the only radiation source that I know of around here is that old weapons cache that we sealed up years ago. Let’s make a quick stop there and see if that’s the source of all of this.”

Putting on the suits, they flew up to the weapons site. As they approached the site, the radiation levels rose and by the time Alec had set down the airship, the levels were at lethal levels with only an hour or so of exposure. Entering the storage area, it was immediately apparent what the problem was. One of the cement casings for the missiles had a large crack in it.

“How’s that possible?” Robert said. “We made these casings a foot thick. The radiation levels are much higher now than they were then too.”

“Could it be because of the heat buildup inside the containers? Maybe that weakened the cement.”

“Possible, I guess.”

“Look at this!” Alec said as pointed to a piece of cement that had broken away. A reddish powder could be seen on the edge of a perfectly cylindrical hole that was drilled in it.

“What in the heck?” Robert said. “Let’s pack that in one of the radiation proof containers over there and take it back with us. I’ll have to test it, but if I had to guess right now I’d say that the powder is thermite and the hole it’s in confirms that this was no accident.”

"Who?" Alec asked.

"Your dad, of course," Robert said. "Finally getting his revenge from what I did to Epoch over a decade ago."

****

The invasion of Epoch and the southern villages was quick. With several hundred paratroopers coming in the middle of the night, the towns were taken without gunfire and before most people even got out of bed.

With complete control of Epoch, including its airport, a military plane from Provenance with Erin aboard arrived late in the morning. As she walked down the ramp from the plane, she was impressed with the military guard assembled ahead of her and the large flag from Provenance fluttering in the wind on a nearby flagpole. After getting an update on the takeover operation and congratulating the general who was in charge, Erin headed towards the town hall.

When Erin entered Jake's office, she saw Jake at his desk with an armed Provenance guard on either side.

"What's the meaning of all of this?" Jake bellowed.

"Good morning, Jake. Fine day, isn't it?" Erin said. "My name is Erin."

"Your general has already filled me in on the details of this little takeover of yours. It won't work you know, unless you plan on keeping thousands of soldiers here to keep us in line."

"It's already worked and I've no intention of keeping a large military presence here. Look Jake, I've no aspirations for world domination, but we needed to put a stop to your culture before it engulfed us. I see many great things here in Epoch and the rest of the Alliance that I'd like to keep just as they are—you, for one."

Jake looked surprised. "Me?"

"Yes, I can tell a good leader when I see one, and after following your activities over the radio for many years, I'd like you to continue managing this town for me. Pretty much like you've done before but with my guidance and rules."

"I can imagine. What rules?"

"Simple ones," Erin said as an aide passed Jake a piece of paper. "As we speak, the leaders of the other villages of your Alliance are receiving the same information that you are receiving."

Jake quickly read through the page. The first part described the takeover that had just taken place; near the bottom of the sheet were the new rules.

1. No livestock of any kind.
2. Quotas will be set for the capture of wild animals and fish.
3. Most of the diet is to be switched to vegetarian.
4. No elections or elected officials.
5. Alliance currency will be replaced with Provenance currency.
6. No use of fertilizers, herbicides, or pesticides.
7. Much tighter emission controls on vehicles and factories.

"Now Jake, you can come out of here looking like a rose and have even more power than when you went to bed last night. That is if you're as smart as I think you are and accept the position of governor of this state, reporting directly to me."

"And if I refuse?"

"Don't mistake my mild manner or gender with softness. If you refuse, I'll have you removed and you'll have the choice of death or moving away from here, which was the same choice that was given to your military commander."

"Jordan? What've you done with him?"

"I don't need to worry too much here if I've got control of the military. I've replaced him and some other key positions with men of my own. I'll also keep extra men here to ensure that the transition of power has no issues, but strongly loyal men at the top is all I need."

"But Jordan?"

"He opted to move up to Percipience instead of getting a bullet in the brain. He and a young lady friend will be leaving shortly for there in one of your, I mean *my*, planes under armed guard and once dropped off, the plane will return here."

"Well, I see little choice in the matter," Jake said. "I'll accept this governorship posting that you're offering to me."

"Excellent!" Erin said. "Now for the first order of business, I want you to do a radio and television address to your Alliance at noon today explaining what has happened and the new rules.

"That's only thirty minutes from now. The people need to know it is coming and I need more time to prepare."

Erin disregarded Jake's protests and motioned her aide to give another set of papers to Jake. She turned around and started to leave the office. She paused at the doorway and looked at Jake.

"My men have been passing the word along all morning to the general population that an announcement will be made at noon. As for you needing time to get ready, there's your speech and I expect you to follow it word for word."

15 ACCLIMATION

Epoch Times – December 14, 2232

The first week of the transition of governments over to Provenance has not been without problems. Starting with yet another currency change, the second in less than a year, which has led to widespread confusion on posted prices on products and what currency is accepted at each store. Some stores are not accepting the new currency yet and others are only accepting the new, leading to frustration amongst shoppers. The one saving grace is that the exchange rate is fixed between the new currency (Young Alliance Worldwide Note or YAWN), the last currency (Fair Alliance Region Treasury or FART) and the old currency (Banknote for Unified Regional Payment or BURP) at 1:2:4.

****

Robert was sitting on a log outside of town hall at Port Aspire. The sun was beginning to set and none too soon as it had been a very warm day. The last week had been hectic with the logistics of moving everyone along with critical items from Percipience to Port Aspire. He had sent word to all of the elders that they would be meeting later in the week. He also told them that nothing major was to be done until then. Critical shelters could be built and food gathered but that was it. It was time to think and plan; it was not time for action.

What he needed to figure out was what Erin was up to. Though he initially blamed Jake for the explosion at the military site, it took only a day to find out that Epoch had also been taken over. With this information, the only conclusion that Robert could come up with was the Erin had also targeted Percipience. But when confronted with the allegation, Erin flatly denied it, which did not make any sense, but then again neither did the attack on Percipience in the first place. And it was an attack. Shortly after arriving at Port Aspire, Robert confirmed his suspicions that the red powder they found at the military site was indeed thermite.

Then there was the unexpected arrival of Jordan and Allison who had walked over to Port Aspire from Percipience. Their presence provided its own set of complications for which Robert did not have any time to deal with either. He simply told them that if he heard of any conflict between them and Kimberly, Lauren or Alec, regardless of who started it, he would banish Jordan and Allison from Port Aspire.

A commotion in the town center brought Robert back to the real world. He saw a growing crowd in the town center that were all pointing and looking up. He looked up and saw Alec's airship going slowly over the town at a low altitude. Tethered below it was large bizarre looking contraption that Robert could not even fathom the purpose of. The airship was heading towards the beach and Robert joined the group of people following it to see what was going on.

When he reached the cove, the cargo had already been set down on the beach and untied from the airship, which was now hovering over the water nearby. Robert could make out Clyde disembarking from the airship and running up to the beach. Once there, he called out for help and soon two large hoses ran from the object to several yards into the water. By the time Clyde finished with the hoses, Robert had made it to the strange device.

"Clyde! What are you up to? I haven't seen you for the last few days."

"I figured my time would be better spent building this."

"But what is it?"

"Give me a few minutes to unfold it and turn it on."

Clyde moved quickly around the object, moving some pieces and locking others into place. When he was done, he came back to Robert who was smiling since he had now figured out what it was.

"Did you want the honors of turning it on?" Clyde asked.

"No, this is all your thing."

Clyde flipped a switch that turned on a series of pumps that began taking water out of the ocean and pushing it into the contraption. Soon, water was running down slides and through misters and sprinklers that were situated in several spots.

"A mini water park. What a great idea!" Robert said after watching the first people from the crowd starting to climb stairs and ladders to get to the top of the slides.

"I thought it would be," Clyde said.

A small shot of water hit Robert in the chest. He looked up and saw one of the kids playing with a water gun that was built into the structure and laughing hysterically. Robert made a fist and then shook it in an exaggerated fashion at the boy, which made the boy laugh even harder and fire another blast at him.

"Nice work," Robert said as he patted Clyde on the back.

"It was nothing to build with this nanotube material. With the jelly fish and rocky bottom, this cove isn't too conducive for playing in. The forced migration from Percipience, the cramped quarters here at Port Aspire, and this horrible heat made me assume that people would enjoy some cool down and play time. I thought this would provide a good distraction for a little while."

After a run down one of the slides himself, Robert knew exactly what other kind of diversion he needed, and so he headed over to the Fabrication hub where he found Alec and other machinists working away.

Sweat was coming off of Alec's brow.

"How goes the radio dish?" Robert asked.

"Coming along pretty well. I managed to snag the radio from the warehouse during the evacuation, but some of the pieces were not stored too well and need to be rebuilt. I think we have the motors and gears now setup to be able to move the dish to keep it aligned with a specific place in the sky. Hopefully the electronics are all still working. We're going to test them out before trying to reach out to Conner. Overall, it should be ready in about a week or so."

****

Jake decided that this was a good opportunity to get some much needed sleep as he closed his eyes and listened to the steady drone of the plane engines. The days in the last week had been full between dealing with the transition of power to Provenance and working with the new commander of the DC. Jake had to also start implementing the changes to the food supply for the mandatory vegetarian diet and now a spur of the moment trip to Provenance to meet with Erin.

Jake was still trying to figure Erin out. During the last week he had spoken to her regularly and she seemed to be fair, but Jake did not trust her. The day that Erin took over Epoch, Jake had heard back from the research team up in Percipience that a radiation cloud had enveloped the town, forcing an evacuation. The timing was too much to be a coincidence and Erin had to be behind it. But what Jake could not figure out is why would Erin want to take out Percipience yet only take over Epoch? It just didn't make any sense.

Jake awoke when the plane touched down in Provenance. As he disembarked from the plane, the heat and humidity hit him hard.

"You should have been here the last few days," said the young private who was escorting Jake to a line of trucks. "A cyclone came through here. Did a bunch of damage too. That's why it's so humid and hot right now."

They walked up to the closest truck and the private gave Jake the keys. "You know how to get to Erin's house?"

"You're not going to come along?"

"No. I was told to give you the keys and directions if you needed them."

"I can find my way," Jake said as he started the truck up and headed out. There were detours setup due to the storm, but he eventually found his way to Erin's place. He was stopped at the front door by two burly guards and after a pat down, was allowed to enter.

"Welcome Jake!" Erin said. "I'm glad you could make it."

"Did I have a choice?"

Erin chuckled. "No, I guess you didn't. But I'm still glad to see you. I've heard good things about you from the commander of the DC. He says you're tackling things like a pro."

"There's a lot to be done."

"There's one point that he said you've made no progress on at all though and that's the modifications that I've requested for your education system."

Jake shook his head. "Yeah, he's right. I'm having a hard time with that. It's wrong."

Erin looked up towards Jake. "Did you say *wrong?*"

"Yeah, I sure did. Look Erin, I know how to be a good soldier, but this plan you want implemented is flawed."

"In what way? We've been using it here in Provenance for decades and everything seems to be working fine. Look at our grade point average; it is nearly forty percent higher than yours."

"That's because you give kids grades for just showing up in class or a minimum grade for turning anything in. You have a policy that rewards kids for trying, not for results. Heck, the teachers aren't even allowed to give a zero percent under your policy. Instead, they have to praise the students even if they really haven't earned it."

Erin was taken back by Jake's directness. "The purpose of the grade is to determine achievement and to not muddle it up with behavior. Just because a student doesn't turn in an assignment doesn't mean that they don't know the material. Besides, if a student is late with an assignment and gets a zero on it, they would lose motivation. Look at our graduation rate. It's higher than yours."

"And you believe what you're saying? All you're doing here is building up false self-esteem in the kids and that will carry over to adulthood. They'll expect to be rewarded even if what they do is late or incomplete. They'll get a greater sense of entitlement and expect to get things without having to put in the effort for them. In other words, they'll have unearned or undeserved demands on their employers, government, and society."

"Look Jake, I'm not going to argue about this. Implement the same policy that we have here. End of discussion."

Jake looked at Erin and knew that this battle was one that he was not going to win. "Alright. I will, but the long-term consequences of this are going to be scary."

****

Allison and Jordan were sitting under a large tarp that had been setup at Port Aspire to offer some shade from the bright sunlight. "I can't handle this heat much longer," she said to Jordan as she waved a fan at her face in a futile attempt to cool down.

An older couple walked past them and glared as there were no more places to sit.

They both ignored the disapproving look. "We could go for another dip in the ocean or check out the contraption that Clyde built," Jordan offered.

"No, I'm done with getting stung by jelly fish and I'd rather sweat for a while more before I join the crowd on Clyde's thing."

Jordan nodded in agreement. "If our plan for Percipience hadn't worked as well as it did, we'd be there instead of here. It's been tough—first the week long walk out here and then nothing but the bare essentials. It just isn't fair. Staying here isn't going to be much fun."

"We simply can't stay here!" Allison said. "During the week that we've been here that witch and her Hive have been manipulating us so much I'm starting to feel like a zombie."

"Me too. Maybe we should talk to Robert and see if he can get her to lighten up on us."

"It's worth a shot. The worst that he can say is no."

They found Robert in the town hall mulling over some paperwork. "What do you two want?" he asked. "I was just going to go and find you."

"We came to talk to you about Lauren," Jordan said.

"That's what I was going to talk to you about too," Robert said. "Over the last week, Lauren has been hardly able to sleep. She keeps getting woken up in the middle of the night because of danger signals from the Hive. Signals that have all been traced back to one of you."

"You don't have to remind us," Allison said. "We're not sleeping that well either with our thoughts being constantly manipulated."

"Basically, I don't see how having the two of you here is going to work out," Robert said. "So, as I told you when you first arrived, if this isn't going to work, I'm going to have to banish you from Port Aspire."

"Banish us!" Jordan said. "That's not fair! We've done nothing wrong and haven't even spoken to Alec, Kimberly, or Lauren. You should tell Lauren to ease up on us."

Robert looked surprised at the request. "Well, that isn't going to happen. I also can't see how this will ever work with the unfound hatred that both of you have."

Allison was about to add to Jordan's protest but Robert held up his hand. "I've made a call to Erin, the leader of Provenance. I've convinced her to take both of you in. She's sending over a plane this afternoon to fly you back to Epoch where you can pick up your things that you left behind. From there you'll get on a transport plane over to Provenance."

Allison's eyes lit up and she looked at Jordan. "From the gossip I've heard, Provenance is huge and they have stores!"

"Yeah, it's got size. Erin is probably going to set us up with our own place to live too. Without parents or anyone else, like it should be," Jordan added as they turned around and left Robert.

Robert watched the two leave and did a small shake of his head. "You're welcome." He said in a soft voice before getting back to work.

****

The evening meeting with the elders at Port Aspire was pretty glum. Though they had taken care of immediate needs, Port Aspire was in no way ready to support an extra couple of thousand people.

"It's not repairing the radiation leak or maybe re-building a whole village that's bothering me," Robert said to the group. "It's the long-term viability of our community and culture. It's clear now that the Hive can't protect us against all things. If someone takes an action that's not directly against us, the Hive does not detect it. Any suggestions?"

"Well, we could build some weapons."

"No! That'll result in us becoming more like them. There must be some way for us to live in peace without constantly being threatened."

There were no other suggestions and the meeting adjourned with the only thing being agreed upon was the activities over the next few weeks to make things livable in the overcrowded Port Aspire.

After the meeting, Robert headed towards the Fabrication hub and found Alec and Clyde tinkering with the radio dish while Heather was sitting beside him but clearly losing patience with her dad.

"Just a little bit longer, sweetie, and then we'll be able to talk to Jeremy," Alec said.

"But I already can talk to him!" the five-year-old explained.

"But the rest of us can't, and I really need to talk to his dad."

"Ok," Heather said as she rolled her eyes and gave a facial expression that only a five-year-old could give.

"Jeremy says that his dad says that they're sending a signal now. But he is saying something about no pictures."

"We'll have to wait for a while," Alec said. "Unlike telepathy, which appears to be instantaneous, our radio waves travel at the speed of light and that carrier signal will take fifteen minutes to get here."

"But how do you know that telepathy is faster than that?" Robert asked.

"Watch. Heather, ask Jeremy what the color of dirt is."

Heather responded right away. "He said that's a silly question. It's red. What other color would it be? But Jeremy is the one being silly because everyone knows that dirt is black!"

"Not on Mars, sweetie," Alec replied.

Alec put a set of headphones on and started to move some dials on the radio dish control panel. After a few minutes, he took the headphones off and flipped a switch that turned the speaker on and the carrier signal could be heard followed by a man's voice. "Hello, Port Aspire! This is Conner from the Mars colony, Noria."

Alec did a high-five with Clyde. "It works! Let's hope we have the tracking stuff right so that we hold onto that audio signal. Like Heather said, I'm not detecting any video," Alec said.

"Noria?" Robert said. "What kind of name is that?"

Clyde shook his head. "That's pretty funny. Think about it for a second."

Robert smiled. "I got it; I just wasn't expecting an anagram."

With the delay, the dialog with Mars was painfully slow. Robert and Alec used a combination of radio and Heather to talk with Jeremy's dad. Heather for the easy-to-understand questions and words and then more detailed information through the radio.

They discovered that the Mars base, Noria, was thriving with a population of fifteen hundred, and they had built a large underground city. Most of their food was grown in the caves as the radiation and atmosphere topside was not conducive to growing crops. Robert reciprocated by going through the basics of Percipience and Port Aspire and outlined the issues that they were having with both Provenance and Epoch.

"It's too bad that we can't leave all of this economics and consumerism here and live with you," Robert added to the end of his last message and then released the transmit button.

"Well, that may be possible," Clyde commented, causing all heads to turn towards him.

Clyde looked at them. "Didn't you all read through Richard's journal? Near the end of it he talks about the last few flights out to Mars and that he arranged for packing up the proto-type ship."

"Can we go visit Jeremy?" Heather asked to no one in particular.

"But that was two hundred years ago; it'll be useless now," Alec said.

"Probably, but maybe not. It sounds like after the Great Loss, he worked with the people at the spaceport in Europe who were vaccinated against the virus to put the proto-type in long-term storage."

"Where?"

"You could have read this all yourself," Clyde said with attitude. "They flew the spaceplane to some place called S-4. I guess that location had a combination of the desert climate plus some big underground storage facility, which was perfect for the long-term storage of it."

"Why didn't you tell us before?"

"Well, if you had read his journal, you'd have known. There are all kinds of interesting things in there."

****

"Heather said that they're talking about a spaceplane," Jeremy said to his dad.

"Unreal!" Conner said and then listened to Robert's radio message that was just arriving, confirming that they were indeed looking for a spaceplane. Conner carefully thought through his response, first giving his sympathy for crisis at Percipience and then excitement over the potential of an intact spaceship. He finished his transmission by saying that he would get a team together to start evaluating what it would take to get Noria's landing strip operational and the planning for their resupply needs.

"It sounds like they have their own set of problems though with those other towns," Jeremey said.

"Yeah, I'll have to get more details on that from Robert, specifically around the cultural differences. But their problems seem, at least on the surface, to be far smaller than ours," Conner said and then turned and looked directly at Jeremy and became quite serious. "Jeremy, it'll be important that you're careful on what information you pass on to Heather. If she asks too many questions about us, distract her by telling her about your pets or something. After all she's very young. We need to have Robert focused on getting here and I don't want her to give him any doubts or suspicions."

16 S-4

Alec had a hard time sleeping ever since Clyde had brought up the topic of the spaceplane. *Even if we find it, would it be still able to fly? Could I even learn how to fly it?*

He'd read the section of Richard's journal referring to the spaceplane a dozen times, but there were few details other than it was stored at an obscure location called S-4. On his next trip over to Percipience, Alec stopped by the computer hut and did some searches. He came up with a little bit of information on the Mars mission and even less when it came to the spaceplanes used for it. In desperation he did a search on S-4, which resulted in a pile of irrelevant articles. He finally tried searching "S-4" and "hangar" and was surprised at the summary of the first link that came up.

Secret government facility close to Area-51 called Section 4 or S-4. Located beside Papoose Lake...

Scanning through the document, he found out that Area-51 was a top secret military complex before the Great Loss with plenty of unconfirmed rumors of prototype airplanes and alien spacecraft being kept there. In addition to the hangars at the base, there was also rumored to exist underground hangars buried within the mountains near the dry Papoose lakebed, about thirty miles away. This area was called section 4 or simply S-4.

It did not take too much effort to convince Clyde that they should make a trip to the rumored caverns, within a week they were prepared for their trip

Robert caught up to them as the *Fly About Thing* was hovering near the dock at Port Aspire, and the young men were putting a portable fusion reactor in the cargo bay.

"With all of the documents talking about underground facilities, we thought we'd better bring more than just lanterns," Alec said. "This reactor and the portable lights should do the trick."

"Probably a good plan," Robert said. "I've been thinking about this trip of yours. Would you mind doing a little extra flying for me before heading to Area-51?"

"Dude, as long as I get out of this heat, I'll do anything you want," Clyde replied while wiping some sweat from his brow.

"I'm game. Where do you have in mind?" Alec asked.

"Other than our trip to Provenance, we haven't travelled more than a few hundred miles from here. I'd like to know how the rest of this continent is doing and compare that to the predictions that are in WISE due to climate change. So instead of going straight to Nevada, I'd like you to do a bit of a zigzag tour to the East Coast first and record what you see."

"Cool," Clyde said. "I'll do a bit of research on WISE to see what things used to look like so I have something to compare to. So, you're not coming on this trip then?"

"Can't. With all of the activity here, both Alec and I can't both be gone that long. Besides, I want to have more discussions with Conner on Noria."

It took a couple of extra days to plan the course, load up extra supplies, and do the research on WISE, but finally Clyde and Alec were ready for their trip. The first days of the flight were uneventful as the *Fly About Thing* cruised over the large forests leading up to the Rocky Mountain range. Though it was early spring, most of the mountain tops had no snowpack and glaciers that had existed two hundred years ago had vanished. Once over the mountains, they came across the central plains where they expected to see grasslands and forest but instead they saw vast expanses of dry dirt and sand dunes.

"You know, the virus that caused the Great Loss was horrible. But if it hadn't occurred, there would've been a Great Loss anyhow," Clyde said. "If the rest of the planet is like this dust bowl, then there would never have been enough food around to feed everyone."

"No kidding," Alec said. "It's a kind of depressing."

They spent several days over the northern region of the continent where there was much more vegetation and wildlife. They also spotted several small villages, all smaller than Percipience. They were excited when they spotted the first one and attempted a landing but when they were close to the ground, someone from the village started shooting at them, forcing an abrupt climb to a higher altitude. Alec was glad that the nanotube fabric was bullet proof; he refrained from attempting any other landings.

The East Coast was where dramatic change could be seen. The large cities that existed there prior to the Great Loss were in the expected state of decay and were mostly under water. With some rough calculations, Clyde determined that the ocean level had risen by at least fifty feet, and this was confirmed when they travelled south and found most of Florida submerged in water.

Their return journey to Nevada went without incident, and after flying over the remains of Las Vegas, it was not too hard to find the Area-51 site. Though there were plenty of sand drifts on it, a long runway still stood clearly out as they approached the site. Landing near the main complex, the young men found most of the buildings to be in good shape, mostly due to the dry desert conditions and military strength construction.

"We should've gone straight to S-4 and not stopped here," Alec said as they started to explore the main administration building and came upon a huge document room. "It's going to be hard to leave with all of the things to find and discover here. My flashlight doesn't even reach the end of this room."

"No kidding. Come over here," Clyde said as he stood by an open elevator door.

"I wouldn't step inside it if I were you," Clyde said when Alec approached. "We don't know how strong the cables are. Lean in though and take a look at the buttons."

Alec peered inside and shone some light on the control panel. "Heck, the floor numbers go to forty. How's that possible? This building is only three stories tall."

"This elevator goes down. There must be a massive underground complex here."

They continued to explore along the main hallway until Alec stopped and turned off his light and told Clyde to do the same. With the hallway plunged into darkness, a faint light could be seen under a doorway ahead of them.

"Must be a window or skylight," Clyde said.

"Cant' be. This is in the middle of the building," Alec said as he turned his flashlight back on.

The two men approached the door. It was a double metal door with ornate metal work on the surface. A plaque beside the door read "Exhibition Hall." The door was locked solid and did not give any movement to Alec's repeated attempts. "Must be electronic locks that are set to lockdown if the power is off," he said pointing to the dead keypad beside the entrance.

"Probably," Clyde said. "I'll be back in a sec."

Clyde returned carrying an axe that he found beside a fire extinguisher at the front of the building. He put down his flashlight and lifted the axe over his head.

"You're going to cut through the metal door with an axe?"

"No man. But I think this might work."

He then swung the axe down hard at the wall that was next to the door. The axe dug into the wall and into the drywall and studs. Several wild swings later and with help from Alec pulling away the debris, they had a hole that they could crawl through. A dim blueish-green light came through the hole and lit up the hallway.

"Well, at least my radiation monitor isn't triggering," Clyde said as he shimmied through the hole. Once inside, he went over to the door and opened it. "The other failsafe is that someone can't get locked in here," he said while holding the door open for Alec.

Alec entered the room which was filled with odd light. The room was large and was like a museum with five exhibits in glass cases. In the center of the room was the source of the light: two small cubes within a glass case. Clyde read the plaque on the case.

Artifacts of unknown purpose found at Alaska crash site – April 1, 2021

"Alien technology?" Alec asked.

"Gotta be, man. Holy crap."

They took a look at the other exhibits, which consisted of photographs of alien-looking ships and pieces of hardware that Alec had not seen before.

"Look, we're going to be coming back here soon," Alec said. "This time with way more people and lights to examine this whole place. But we really should be getting out to S-4 to see if the spaceship is for real or not."

"Ok, but I'm taking these along," Clyde said, pointing to the glowing cubes. He opened the glass case and then gingerly touched one of the cubes. The glow intensified slightly. Finally, he gathered up the courage to pick them up and wrapped them in the cloth that they were sitting on.

At the first ray of sunshine the next morning, Alec piloted the airship southwest of the complex and soon came upon the mountain range that he thought the hangars would be at. Within a few passes, they found three manmade entrances near the base of the mountain. They landed the airship nearby and walked over to one. The entrances were easily wide enough for a plane to go through and had a large metal door for the main entrance; there was also a small normal-sized side door at the edge.

A crowbar and sledgehammer quickly opened up the corroded side entrance door. Upon going through the door, they turned on their lanterns and saw that the tunnel from the entrance ran for a quarter of a mile before opening into a vast chamber.

Alec and Clyde shone their lanterns around and saw various planes and vehicles in various states of decay. Layers of dust and rocks were on the ground that must have fallen from the cavern ceiling.

"We'll have to come back here with a crew and do a salvage operation. There are tons of books and materials here that we could really make use of," Alec said. "But this is not what we came for; let's try the next entrance."

Repeating the same procedure on the side entrance for the next hangar, they were not surprised when they entered and saw the tunnel stretch into the mountain like the first one had. They sprinted down to the end of the tunnel and found a much smaller cavern at the end that contained more planes and vehicles. They started to walk to the end of the cavern while shining their lanterns around to inspect what was there. Suddenly Clyde stopped as he pointed his lantern to one of the back corners of the cavern.

"Is that it?" Though the light from his lantern could not show the whole vehicle, they could see that it was an odd-shaped craft.

"Could be," Alec said as they moved quickly over to the craft. It was unlike any plane that Alec had seen before with a cigar shape about the size of a bus and only small wings. Alec put a hand on the exterior.

"These feels like nanotube fabric," he said as he moved towards a ramp near the back of the craft.

The inside of the structure was even more foreign to the men than the exterior was. The rear of the craft was lined with vertical coffin-like cylinders with clear doors.

"These must be the sleeping pods," Clyde said. "But there is no privacy at all—kind of strange."

Alec was examining some devices beside the pods. "These must be for food or the latrine, but I've no idea how they work."

They continued to the front of the craft and entered the cockpit area. There were four chairs in front of the instrument panels.

"Have you noticed that there are no windows at all?" Alec asked. "I've not seen a single sign or label with any writing on it in this entire ship either."

Clyde sat down in one of the chairs, which was too big for him. "Alec, I'm getting this creepy feeling that this is a spaceship alright, but it is definitely not one of ours."

"What do you mean?"

"I mean this is a real alien ship. It has to be. There's nothing in here that I can relate to, and look at these chairs. They're not designed for us."

Alec took a good look at the chairs and realized that instead of four chairs, there was really only two. "My God, you may be right. They are like if you took a normal chair, cut it in half and then put a foot separation between the two halves. A real alien ship—can you imagine?"

The two young men finished their exploration of the ship and then did a walk around the rest of the hangar.

"We need to come back here for sure, but I'm not seeing Richards's spaceplane," Alec said.

"There's one more hangar," Clyde said. "Let's check that one out."

The third hangar was similar to the second with a small cavern at the end of the tunnel, but this time, the men knew that they had hit pay dirt, for in the middle of the cavern was a huge rectangular room encased in clear plastic. With only the lanterns it was hard to see everything inside the room, but what they could make out was a craft that looked very much like a big high-tech plane.

The men approached the room and found a doorway whose edges had been sealed with some compound. A sign beside the door confirmed that they had found what they were looking for.

This is an argon-filled structure designed to protect the spaceplane within. Do not open this doorway unless authorized.

"Do I've your authorization to open this?" Clyde said as he approached the door with a knife.

Alec laughed. "Go for it. Only open it slightly though; I don't want to pass out from breathing that stuff in. Then let's go back to the airship and get the fusion reactor and some proper lights to light up this whole cavern. By the time we're done with that, there should be enough normal air in there for us to breathe."

After they returned and setup lights around the perimeter of the room, they were able to see the enormity of the plastic shell room and the spaceplane within it. They cautiously entered the room. With full light now, they were able to see that in addition to the spaceplane, there was also a stack of crates behind it.

The spaceplane itself was similar in shape to the passenger jets that existed prior to the Great Loss with some exceptions. The first difference was two large cylinders that were mounted to the fuselage and were the length of the plane. Other major differences included the stubbier wings and the entrances to both the passenger and cargo areas, which were underneath the body instead of on the side. Near the front of the ship, the words *Serene Trip* were written in a large Cyrillic font.

"Nice anagram for a spaceship," Clyde said.

The two men walked under the plane and started to head up the ramp that led up into the passenger area of the craft. Once inside, they turned their lanterns back on and began to explore, starting with the cockpit.

"This is more like it," Alec said seeing the two padded chairs that faced a complex instrument panel.

"Just a little more complicated than your airplane in Epoch, huh?"

"Yeah," Alec said nervously as he gazed at each bank of gauges, switches, and keyboards. *What was I thinking? There's no way that I'll be able to fly this.*

Clyde examined a clipboard that was in a pouch behind one of the seats. "Ah a flight log. Looks like this has flown about thirty times with all of the landings at the European Space center. It was brought here after the first manned expedition to Mars was launched."

"Well, that lines up with Richard's journal. The virus was right around that time and he had this brought here in the off chance that they may need it later on. But I don't think he was thinking of two hundred years later."

Giving up on trying to understand anything from the control panel, the men went to the back of the plane where they found six seats that looked similar to the ones in the cockpit along with a small galley, exercise area, plenty of storage compartments and a washroom.

"Pretty small area to live in for a trip to Mars. How long do you think the flight would be?" Clyde asked.

"I read on WISE that the average trip took eight months. It varies depending on the position of the planets. I was hoping to find some manuals around here on how this works, but so far nothing."

"Maybe they're in the cargo areas or in those crates outside."

The cargo area proved to be empty, so the two men left the spaceplane and headed over to the stack of crates.

"There must be over a hundred crates here!" Clyde said.

Alec walked to the center of the stack and on one of the crates was a clear envelope that allowed Alec to read the top piece of paper that it contained.

Packing List

1. Maintenance data discs
2. Engineering data discs
3. Flight simulator
4. Flight suits

The list went on with what appeared to be a series of spare parts for the spaceplane.

"Jackpot!" Alec yelled to Clyde. "You and I are going to become astronauts!"

****

Conner was whistling a happy tune, a tricky thing to do in a spacesuit, as he drove the large dump truck down the red dirt road towards the processing plant. Calling the vehicle a truck was an exaggeration as it really was just a collection of parts from one of the original spaceships. With an open cab, metal wheels, and part of the spaceship hull as the truck bed, it was not pretty, but was functional.

The reason that Conner was so happy was that he had found out that the men from Earth had found a spaceship kept in long-term storage. Though they indicated that a lot of work needed to be done and that there was no guarantee that they would attempt a flight to Mars, they were going to start the preparation for it.

One of the conditions for the flight would be to ensure that there was enough fuel and other supplies stored at Noria for the ship's return back to

Earth. Conner assured them that there would be, and this was the reason he was out this morning hauling extra loads of Martian soil to the processing plant.

I'll have the methane, oxygen, and water ready in time to refuel the ship. After all, it'll be at least two years before the ship arrives. But what's more important is to get Jeremy ready if they do come. I'm going to have to double up on his medication for sure and start preparing a list of supplies from Earth that Noria desperately needs.

17 PREPARATION

"So what do you think after being here for a year?" Erin asked Jordan, who she had summoned to see at her home.

"Both Allison and I are really enjoying it. She's fitting in well at your university and I'm enjoying being a full-time pilot in your military. It's much less pressure than being the head of the Defense Center in Epoch."

"Ha!" Erin said. "I'm sure it is."

"Your city is about four times the size of Epoch too, so that means more of everything. More to do, more places to shop and the like."

"Even more so when compared to Port Aspire," Erin said. "This is why I asked you to come here today. I was talking to your former boss, Jake, the other day about the defenses of both of our towns and he made an offhand remark that I keep thinking about."

"What did he say?"

"He made the comment that we should start up the genetic pairing here to build up a defense system like Port Aspire has. I know that some of the people over there have some limited psychic abilities but a psychic defense shield? You don't believe that do you?'

"It's real! Both Allison and I've had first- or second-hand experience with it. It's their only defense since weapons, other than those for hunting, are actually forbidden there."

"No weapons at all? I was wondering about that when they came here a year ago. They had no security people at all. I wrote it off at the time, thinking that with his size, Robert probably didn't think he needed any."

"Who was part of that visit?"

"Let's see, there was Alec, Robert, and a younger man—a bit of an odd fellow."

"Clyde."

"Yes, that was his name, and then Lauren and her daughter."

"With Lauren around, Robert was safe. She's the head of the Hive, and I doubt if your entire army could have got to him if they tried."

"She's that powerful?"

"Yes, and the scary part of the story is that I've heard that her daughter is far stronger."

"Hmm, maybe I've underestimated them."

"You don't have a thing to worry about. They're not trying to take over the planet, and they are quite content to have their small villages."

"No threat now but things change. You never know what will happen if they get a new leader or what will happen when Lauren's daughter grows up and then wakes up in a bad mood one day."

Jordan nodded. "Yeah, I guess that's true. There's a weakness in the Hive, though."

Erin's eye widened. "A weakness?"

"Yes. The Hive triggers on the detection of any direct attack on the town or its people. They then flood the source of the aggression with thoughts that make it impossible for the attack. But if the attack isn't directly against the village, then it goes undetected. There's also a range limitation of about fifty miles or so."

"Interesting. So if someone were to trigger say a radiation cloud and it floated over their town, they couldn't stop it," Erin said, looking directly at Jordan.

Jordan could not stop a small smile coming across his face. "Exactly."

****

There were three different alarms going off at the same time, and the console was filled with red flashing lights. Alec's palms were sweating as his eyes darted from one reading to the next trying to determine what to do. He did not have to look at any instrument to know that he did not have much time. Glancing up, he saw the red planet's surface approach quickly.

Knowing that he was coming in much too fast and at too shallow of an angle, he tried to angle the ship higher by pulling back on the control stick, but it was too little too late. He could make out fine details of the rocks on the surface as the ship overshot the runway and crashed.

"Dang it!" Alec said as he leaned back in the flight chair. He had spent the last two days in the flight simulator trying to handle the manual landing of the spacecraft with limited success. *Thankfully, the ship has enough smarts to take off and land on its own, and I should never have to do this for real. I'm also really glad that whoever designed it didn't have it rely on satellites or GPS for landings. Instead, the computer listens to three radio beacons that are at the landing site to determine its position and perform perfect landings each time.*

It had been a year since the discovery of the *Serene Trip;* during that time, Alec and Jordan had submersed themselves into learning about spaceflight along with the operation of the spaceship. The spaceplane was designed to take off and land like a normal plane and was powered by methane, a fuel that could easily be manufactured on both planets.

Under the condition that he would get the final say on whether the mission was to proceed, Robert had agreed to lend a few men to help in getting things ready. This included the preflight preparations of the craft, clearing of the runway at Area-51, making the fuel, and gathering other supplies for the mission.

As the chances of a mission increased, Conner sent a list of supplies that were needed in Noria. In addition to the expected list of replacement parts, medical supplies, and raw materials, there was a request for seeds for a variety of plants, both for food and medicine. Port Aspire did not have most of the requested seeds, so Clyde suggested a trip to a pre Great Loss seed bank that was near the North Pole. Taking the *Fly About Thing*, a team led by Kimberly was dispatched and returned with all of the needed seeds plus a welcome surprise for both Robert and Alec: coffee tree seeds!

During the last year, Robert also spent a considerable amount of time speaking to Conner. The more that Robert learned about the red planet and the community that was up there, the more he became convinced that this was the only path that he could lead his village. While the Hive was protecting them now, only the physical barrier of outer space would ensure that the culture of Port Aspire would be safe from the consumption-based one at Epoch and Provenance.

But even with this in mind and the preparation of the spaceplane going well, the decision to make a trip was not an easy one for Robert to make.

"Ok, so you've convinced me that the *Serene Trip* is ready; it has passed all of the diagnostics for a flight," Robert said to Alec. "Combine this with the supplies gathered, the training you and Clyde have done, and the preparation of the fuel and other essentials needed for the trip and I'd agree with you that the trip out there is about as ready as it could ever be."

"So it's a go then?" Alec asked eagerly.

"You're like Conner and just want this flight to happen. But have you thought this through? Suppose we fly out there and take a firsthand look at the planet, infrastructure and community and everything looks great. Then what?"

"What do you mean?"

"How are we going to move this whole village there? The spaceplane only seats eight people, including the pilots, and it sure as heck isn't going to last for the several hundred trips it would take to move everyone, not to mention that a round trip takes over two years to do."

"Clyde and I've been discussing this and we have some thoughts."

"I'm listening."

"We need to understand why we want to move there."

"Well, to get away from the culture of Epoch and Provenance, of course."

"But we, the current people living here at Port Aspire, are under no real threat. The Hive is protecting us. What you're concerned about is future generations and the challenges that they'll have as Epoch and Provenance expand."

Robert thought about this for a moment "Ok, I think I see where you're going on this. Even if something bad happens here on Earth, our way of life will continue on at Noria."

"Exactly. If some future generation of ours gets taken over by the consumption-based culture here on Earth, then there's always Noria."

"I was more thinking of something bad with the environment on Earth, like runaway greenhouse gases making most of the planet unlivable. But regardless of the catastrophe, I understand now. So what's the point of going to Mars at all then?" Robert asked.

"Well, if we're going to count on them for the future of our culture, we need for them not to just survive but to thrive. Though they were well stocked during the initial settlement over two hundred years ago, the plans were for more flights to get more supplies to them. I think we can do a couple of flights over the next several years and bring them those supplies, plus a few people may want to stay there as well."

"Yeah, I've heard Conner say that they don't have much bio-diversity. Different plants, insects, and more animals would be of great benefit to them. They're also in critical need for some medical supplies and replacement machine parts."

"The other reason for going to Mars is Heather."

"What does my granddaughter have to do with it?"

"Lauren is insisting that if we go, Heather joins us. She feels that it's important for Jeremy and her to meet. Something about them being able to make some big breakthrough in psychic abilities with the glowing artifacts that we found at Area-51. My challenge is to make a spacesuit for her. All of the ones that were packed with the spaceship are for adults."

"Can't you make one out of nanotube fabric?"

"That's the plan and then retrofit the air and heat equipment from one of the adult suits to it. I'll get at it; it's just one other thing to get done."

"I'm sure that you will. Just be glad that I'm not going otherwise you'd have to build one for me too since the suits you have are far too small. There's one thing that I can't quite figure out with Conner though."

"What's that?" Alec asked.

"He's talked a fair bit about Mars but he's really interested in Earth and specifically the root of our problems—not only about consuming less but from a psychological viewpoint."

"I wonder why he's interested in that. Communication is tough enough with the time delay, yet he keeps asking questions. What kind of answer or conclusion did you give him?"

"Well, when you boil it all down, it's about people's thinking around entitlement, thinking they deserve things that they haven't earned, not caring about the consequences of their actions and in general not being grateful for what they have. When Conner and I finally got to that point, he seemed excited and hasn't asked about it since."

"That's rather odd," Alec said. "But he seems to have everything under control with enough fuel and other supplies to restock the *Serene Trip* when we get there."

"You sound like you are assuming I'm going to give the okay to this trip."

"Am I wrong?"

Robert paused for a moment. "No, you're not. The mission is a go."

****

Since Jordan and Allison were sent to Provenance, life for Kimberly and her children had calmed down considerably; she spent her free time either helping with the spaceship preparation or working with Robert in the small Port Aspire lab.

"Robert, though this is exhilarating work, I'm failing to see the point. You've already confirmed my analysis on the emissions. Given that, aren't we too late to stop the runaway greenhouse gases?"

"Maybe, but I'm not going to give up that easily. Who knows? Maybe we'll come up with a breakthrough that'll turn the tables."

Robert's plan was to tackle the carbon problem by starting the RECTIFY project (Reduce Extra Carbon to Improve Future Years). The project was really a two-prong attack tackling the greenhouse gasses in the air and the acidification of the oceans. He was hoping that he and Kimberly could design an easy-to-build device to do both that could someday be mass produced.

The overall design was to run a nanotube cable from a shallow ocean floor location to a kilometer in the air where it would be supported by a vacuum balloon. At the top of this cable would be a powerful fan that would drive air through a bio-mechanical device that would separate out the carbon and send it to the ocean floor below via the nanotube. At the ocean surface, a similar type of strategy would be used to remove carbonic acid from the salt water. All of this would be powered either by a windmill or by a cold fusion reactor.

"But even if we could get all of this working and build it full size, it would only remove two, maybe three tons of carbon per week," Kimberly said.

"But what if we could build a thousand or even ten thousand over the next one hundred years? Then we'd start making a difference."

"How could you build so many?"

"If we can get it easy enough to build and working properly, I'm thinking of talking to Erin to see if she would be interested in assisting. Even though I don't agree with their culture, they still care about the environment."

"Erin? Do you still talk to her? I'd heard that she was the one that caused the radiation leak that forced us to evacuate Percipience."

"Yeah, we still talk on a weekly basis. I'm pretty sure it was her, but not certain. Whoever caused the leak at the nuclear missile site went through a lot of work to make it look like a natural failure, but Alec and I found traces of thermite so I know otherwise. Combine that with the timing of the takeover of Epoch and everything points to Erin."

"Did you say thermite?"

"Yes. It wasn't much but I confirmed it with some tests in the lab."

"Oh my! When I started to suspect that something was going on with Jordan, I put a bug in his office and listened to many conversations. That's how I found out about Allison and him. But I also overheard those two talking about thermite, but I had no idea what they were intending to do with it."

"Jordan and Allison? I didn't suspect them!" Robert said. "They wouldn't have been foolish enough to do this on their own, though. Jake must have been in on it to!"

18 DECEPTION

For all of the anticipation and excitement of the trip, the actual flight to Mars was nearly boring. With the computer taking care of all of the controls, the biggest challenge facing the new astronauts was to find something to do on the eight-month journey. Though the spaceplane could handle eight people, the final crew consisted of only Alec, Clyde, Lauren, and Heather with the rest of the ship filled with supplies that Noria requested. The only real complaint came from Clyde who threw a temper tantrum during the first week when he realized that there was no smoking of anything allowed for the duration of the flight.

As they got near the red planet, Alec punched in the computer request for a landing at Noria. The confirmation of the landing beacons came back quickly and the computer notified him that it was taking control for the rest of the flight.

Both Alec and Clyde were in the cockpit when the *Serene Trip* made the final approach to Noria. They spotted the lights from the landing strip as the spaceship performed large sweeping turns to slow its entry speed. As they got nearer, several domes could be seen. They made careful notes on the way that the computer was controlling the descent and final line up with the runway.

"The dang thing makes it look easy," Clyde said.

"No kidding. I think I've only been able to do a good landing about five times in the simulator after at least a hundred tries."

"About the same here."

The red surface quickly approached and with a degree of anti-climax, the *Serene Trip* touched down and coasted to a perfect landing, stopping close to a small dome.

After putting on their spacesuits, they exited the ship. Though the runway had been cleared, red dust rose up with each footstep, and Heather squealed with delight as she jumped nearly six feet in the air.

"Heather! Stop it! We need to be careful in these spacesuits," Lauren said.

"It's hard to resist it," Clyde said. "With the gravity being about a third of that on Earth, I feel like doing the same thing."

Though it was the middle of the day, the outdoor lights from the nearby building were useful as the sun was a small dot overhead in the sky. They saw a figure come out of the dome and head towards them in a tractor.

Though Alec tried to communicate over the radio, there was no response and it was not until the figure had reached them and touched his helmet to his that he could hear him. "You made it! What a landing!" Conner said enthusiastically. "I'm going to pull your ship over to the hangar. I'll meet your team over there and we can unload the critical supplies."

Alec and the rest of the team watched as Conner put the spaceship in the dome and hooked some cables up to it. Conner then motioned for them to an exit on the other side of the dome where a shuttle bus awaited them. Alec and Clyde first went into the cargo area of the *Serene Trip* and picked up a few crates and then joined the lineup to get through the shuttle's small airlock. Once everyone was in the shuttle and had removed their space suits, introductions were done, which included vigorous handshakes and hugs from Conner.

Conner appeared to be at least sixty years old and the impact of growing up on Mars could immediately be seen. In addition to a very pale skin color, the lower gravity resulted in Conner being taller than Alec, but he had far less muscle tissue.

"I'm so excited that you made it here," Conner said. "Sorry for not getting you into the shuttle sooner, but getting your ship into the hangar was important. Without external power, she'd start to freeze up nearly right away; the dome will also protect her from this blasted red sand."

"Where's Noria?" Lauren asked.

"Not too far away," Conner said. "This is the support area for the landing strip. It hasn't been used since the original landings, so it took a while for us to get it back in order." He pointed out one of the side windows of the shuttle. "The solar panels supply the power for this area and the large tanks beside them contain methane, air, oxygen, water and that kind of stuff that you'll need for your return trip."

Conner went to the front of the shuttle and started driving down a trail heading towards a cluster of mountains. "I know that the original plan for Noria was to make domes and live primarily above ground, but that plan was changed about ten years after the original party landed here."

"All underground now?" Clyde asked.

"In caves actually. A series of large ones that were found in the mountains that we're heading for. Living above ground is tough. First you have to build strong buildings to withstand the harsh wind, then there's the radiation shielding that's needed, and after that you have to constantly repair them from punctures from the micro sized meteorites that bombard this planet. We still built the structures, but in the caves instead. Much lighter construction."

"Why build them at all?"

"Try as we might, it was hard to make the caves completely airtight. Plus it is nicer living within the domes. You'll see."

Everyone spent the next few hours looking out of the windows at the reddish-orange sky, endless red sand, and the view of the two moons of the alien world. The ground was flat with the exception of the occasional crater and an abundance of sand ripples that the shuttle happily bounced over.

The flat ground gave way to an incline and soon an entrance to a man-made tunnel appeared. Conner drove carefully into it and stopped the shuttle in front of a large overhead door. Pressing a button on the console, he waited until the door opened revealing a garage area about the size of the shuttle. There was a red flashing light on the wall in front of them. He drove in, pressed another button, and waited until the light went off and a solid green light came on.

"Welcome to Noria," Conner said. "This airlock is fairly new, built only about ten years ago. It avoids us having to suit up again. Please follow me."

"The air smells like roses!" Lauren said as soon as the shuttle door opened.

"The air we make gets circulated through our recreation dome before going through the rest of the complex. That dome has a great deal of vegetation in it and gives the air a fresh smell. I don't even notice it anymore," Conner said and then led the group through a small doorway, down a hallway and into a room with tables and chairs.

"Where's Jeremy and the rest of the Noriaians?" Alec asked.

"Jeremy will be here in a little while," Heather said. "As soon as he," pointing to Conner, "breaks some bad news to us."

"Bad news? I don't like that sound of that," Alec said while looking suspiciously at Conner.

Conner nodded as his jubilant attitude was replaced with a much more sober one while motioning everyone to sit down. "You're not going to like what I've to say. I'm afraid that I've misled you. The only people left here at Noria are myself, about ten others around my age, and Jeremy."

"What!" Alec said with a raised voice. He started to stand up until Lauren coaxed him to sit back down.

"First Provenance and now Noria. Doesn't anyone tell the truth anymore?" Clyde said shaking his head.

"I'm dreadfully sorry for the deception," Conner said. "Everything was going great here until about five years ago when one of our mining expeditions came across a great discovery. Water! Yes, they found a large underground aquifer not far from here. You can imagine how excited we all were since we've had to make all of our water up to that point."

"This doesn't sound so bad," Alec said.

"That's right. At first things were great. We put in a pipeline to the aquifer and turned off our water-making facilities and everything was going smoothly until about a month of regular use. That's when we first started to notice it."

"What?" Clyde said.

"We thought we'd done every conceivable test on the water. We even put it through low level ultra-violet radiation to make sure it was safe, but we obviously missed something. There was a micro-organism in it that went into stasis at cooler temperatures but after a month or so above sixty degrees, it was activated. It's an evil little critter too since it seems to have a taste for carbon."

"Carbon? No living thing lives off of carbon," Alec said.

"Well, that isn't the only thing it consumes, but it does seem to have an appetite for it and considering that the human body is about fifteen percent carbon, you can imagine the results. The micro-organism did not propagate quickly but still within two months, nearly our entire population died."

"That must have been a horrible way to die," Lauren said.

"It was and I've witnessed hundreds of them. All of our crops were infected with the disease as well and had to be destroyed. We removed the soil from the greenhouses and have setup a couple of small new growing areas again. We don't need much food with the few people that are now left."

"How did you, Jeremy, and the others survive?" Clyde asked.

"Luck, I guess if you consider it lucky having to witness everyone around you dying. My best guess is that we must have some specific gene sequence that makes us immune to the little bugger. I've run several tests on the survivors and the micro-organism not only does not activate, it actually disintegrates."

"So, you invite us here so that we could die as well?" Alec asked.

"No, you're perfectly safe. The little monster isn't airborne and seems to like living in liquids. We have switched back to man-made water and with the crops destroyed and soil replaced, I think we have finally eradicated it.

"But why lie to us?" Laruen asked.

"It's too late for me and the other adults to be rescued, but I want you to take Jeremy back to Earth. There are no other children and after we pass away, there would be no life for him here. Would you've come if you knew the truth?"

"That does not matter. You don't have the right to put us in danger both with the trip here and with the risk of being infected."

"I'm sorry, but I couldn't see an alternative."

"Can he even survive on Earth? He's used to much lower gravity," Lauren asked.

"He was only five years old when the outbreak occurred. I've been giving him gene therapy treatments since then to increase his bone density and muscle growth. He has a tough exercise routine and wears weighted clothes, all in the hope that he may someday get a chance to go to Earth."

"Well, it's not that great on Earth either," Alec said. "As you know from your discussion with Robert, there's a constant struggle with other groups who want to return to basically the same way of life like before the Great Loss. Then there is the extreme climate changes that are already leaving many areas of the planet uninhabitable. We were counting on Noria as being the place where our culture could prosper, but that looks like it is out of the question now. We can maybe make one or two more trips here, but it'll be a long time before we're ready to build spaceships to get a settlement going here again."

"Yes, you're right, and even if you were able to, you'd still have to live underground like we are and deal with the killer bacteria," Conner said and then his face lit up. "However, not all is lost! There may be something that I can give you that'll help you with at least one of your problems on Earth."

"What?" Alec asked skeptically.

"We don't want any weapons. That's one of the laws set down from the beginning that we still abide to," Lauren said.

"I'm not talking about a weapon," Conner said. "My specialty and one that's been a concentration here on Mars since we arrived is gene therapy. We needed it in several areas to be able to adapt to the different environment on this planet. At first, we started with simple physical attributes such as better eyesight to cope with the low light conditions outside and getting the body to release more endorphins to make people happier. It does get kind of depressing living underground most of the time."

"So you're proposing that making people happier on Earth will fix everything?" Clyde asked doubtfully. "If that's it, I can do that too."

"No, that was just the beginning. The scientists before me left a foundation of knowledge that I've been working on my entire career. I've taken gene therapy to a whole new level: behavior modification."

"Impossible! Behavior is learned," Alec said.

"Most behavior is, but certain traits in the way we react to things or how we feel can be controlled through genes, especially the primitive ones."

"So, I'm lost; how does this help our problem on Earth?" Alec asked.

"I believe I've developed a drug that will genetically alter a person to feel less entitled to things and more grateful for what they have."

"Dude, that's outrageous! Have you named it yet?"

"No, I haven't."

Just then, Heather stood up and headed to the doorway which opened as she neared it. A boy several years older than her wearing a heavy-looking vest came in.

"Ah, this is Jeremy," Conner said.

Jeremy said a shy hello to everyone and then exchanged a hug with Heather.

"Jeremy, why don't you show Heather your fluffle of rabbits. We have more things to discuss here and then it'll be time to for us to gather for the evening meal and get some rest."

"Rabbits?" Lauren asked as the children left.

"It's the only animal we have here and for some reason they didn't get infected by the bacteria. We've done some genetic modifications to them too; I think you'll be surprised. There were plans to send other animals but there were no more supply ships."

"Got it!" Clyde interrupted.

"Got what?" Alec asked.

"A name for Conner's new drug. I think it should be named the *Hell Turned Ego* cure," Clyde said.

Conner looked at Clyde for a moment, then smiled. "That's perfect!"

Alec had a perplexed look on his face. "I don't get it."

"Dude! Did you skip class when they taught anagrams?" Clyde said while shaking his head. "I'll explain it to you later."

Conner then continued on his discussion regarding the *Hell Turned Ego* cure that he developed and explained that with continuous application, such as through a water supply, it would slowly alter people's behaviors. Though skeptical about the claims, Alec agreed that they would give it a try but said that he had to talk to Robert first before agreeing to take Jeremy back with them.

"Earth will be above the horizon after the evening meal," Conner said as he led them to their sleeping quarters. "You can chat with Robert then. In the meantime, I'm sure that all of you would like to take a hot shower after that long journey."

After the evening meal, everyone felt much better and had a new appreciation for open spaces, hot showers, and real cooked food after their eight-month long voyage. Heather and Jeremy were inseparable and Lauren couldn't keep up with the pace of the telepathic message stream between them.

Conner led Alec to the radio room and then left so that he could talk in private to Robert. There was the usual ten-minute delay in communications so Alec carefully laid out his message so that Robert got the entire picture in one shot. He waited for the ten minutes it took the message to reach Earth and then another ten minutes to get a reply back. It actually took nearly thirty minutes.

"I can hardly believe what you said regarding Noria and that Conner misled us so," Robert said. "This also kind of wrecks the plans that you and I had for Noria being the safe harbor for our culture. I guess we can't trust anyone anymore and that goes double for this miracle cure that Conner is claiming to have developed. We don't know his motive here for making that or what it may do to us if we take it, but I have to admit that it does have a clever name. The micro-organism does interest me and I want you to get a sample of it. If the boy looks strong enough to stand Earth's gravity, then I see no reason why you shouldn't take him back with you. Based on what you've told me, it's the right thing to do."

Alec signed off the radio and headed back to the sleeping quarters. He realized that it had been a long time since he had last slept, well before the landing, and he was exhausted. The only thing that was on his mind was to get some sleep after he got Clyde to explain his latest anagram.

19 REDEMPTION

"But they're not a threat at all!" Jake said raising his voice in Erin's den. He had been summoned to Provenance several times over the three years since Epoch had been expropriated. On each trip, he usually simply agreed with whatever Erin said or wanted but on this occasion he could not.

"Port Aspire may not be a threat now, but it soon could be," Erin said. "Especially with this Hive that they have. I spoke to your former DC commander and he convinced me that they could immobilize our entire army."

"They'd never do that. They're still dealing with the radiation cloud that forced them to move to Port Aspire. I assume that was you that started that since it happened nearly at exactly the same time as the takeover of Epoch."

"Me!" Erin gave out a raspy laugh. "No, it wasn't me. I'm pretty sure it was your own DC commander who was behind that!"

"Jordan?" Jake said and then the pieces started to fall into place—the unexplained trips, the thermite, and the look of guilt that he caught him at once in a while. "I never would've thought that he would cross me like that."

"That's why I run the structure of government that I have here," Erin said. "As a dictator and the head of both the government and the army, I've a better chance at making sure that nobody is plotting against me."

"However, that still doesn't mean you need to finish Port Aspire off."

"I disagree. Better to finish them off now while they're still small than to try to take them on when they get stronger. The plan is to launch a series of missiles from Epoch, and that's why I wanted to speak to you. I want you to make sure that the team that I'm currently sending over to Epoch with the missiles gets your full cooperation."

Jake knew that he had little choice but to agree. "Of course, though I still think it's unnecessary. When are you planning to execute this?"

"Ever since my discussion with Jordan, I've put a rush on the development of some medium-range missiles. The latest two-hundred mile tests went well, so I've had several more prototypes made. They'll be shipped out to Epoch on the same plane that you'll return in along with a team to set them up. They have a lot to do, especially with the guidance systems since we don't have GPS to guide the missiles. Instead, we need to chart the terrain and then program that in so that the missiles will actually hit their intended targets. Overall, we should be ready for the attack within half a year or so."

Jake was lost in thought as he left Erin's office. *My son and grandkids are there. I must put a stop to this somehow or at least warn them.*

✳✳✳✳✳✳✳✳✳✳✳✳✳✳✳✳✳✳✳

The morning following their arrival, Conner found the adult earthlings in the kitchen area. He was curious about the dark fluid that Alec was preparing.

"Tea?" Conner asked.

"No, it's coffee. Pretty addictive, especially in the morning."

"We have tea here. I've only read about coffee."

"Well, we've brought along a crate of the imitation coffee that we make on Earth and some seeds that we just found for real coffee trees. Soon, both of us will be able to have the real thing."

"Heather is still sleeping, I presume?" Conner asked Lauren.

"Yes, she's zonked out and I didn't have the heart to wake her," Lauren said.

"I'm not surprised. I poked at Jeremy a while ago and he's the same way. He mumbled something about them being up most of the night talking, I assume telepathically. I set his alarm to give him some more sleep and told him when it goes off, to wake Heather and meet us at the recreation dome. In the meantime I can give you a tour of the rest of Noria."

The tour started by suiting up in spacesuits for an outdoor trip to see the power, water, and air generation systems. He started with the water extraction system where Martian dirt was brought in, put on a conveyor belt, and then heated by microwaves which vaporized the water contained in the soil.

"Even with all of the recycling we do, it took the equivalent of ten people working full time to get enough water for us," Conner said.

"That's not too bad considering the population of Noria was a few thousand people," Alec said.

"Well, I exaggerated when I told you and Robert that," Conner said. "I wanted it to sound like we were thriving here when in actuality it's been a struggle to survive. Before the disaster, there was only about two hundred people here."

Alec's spacesuit hid the frustration that was on his face as he was reminded of the lies he had been told.

"Well, that puts some perspective around things," Clyde said. "Since you have to make everything from raw materials, it would take a long time to build another machine like this, plus the trucks and loaders. Until you do, you can't really expand your population."

"Exactly. Most of people's time here was devoted to just staying alive," Conner said. "Take me, for example. Though genetics is my specialty, before the disaster, I could only work on it a couple of hours a day. The rest was devoted to tasks involved in keeping this place running, and there were no days off. Thankfully, we have some good equipment in our machine shop like the 3D printer that makes creating parts pretty easy.”

Conner continued the outdoor tour with a walk around the power plant, which was a large collection of solar panels. He explained that the first Mars settlers used batteries to store power for the night time, but that was very limiting and they were hard to build and maintain. To solve this problem, they built up large flywheels to store the energy and they located them in the power station building. After the power station, they did a walk through the facility that created oxygen, nitrogen, methane, and other essential elements.

“We have mines as well,” Conner said as they headed back to the airlock leading into the mountain cavern complex that held the living area of Noria. “We use them as needed for iron, copper, and the like.”

When they were all finished getting through the airlock and had removed their spacesuits, they were greeted by Jeremy and Heather.

“Ah, you two are finally awake,” Clyde said. “We’re going to take a look at the greenhouses. Do you want to come along?”

Heather’s eyes lit up. “You need to see the bunnies!” She then grabbed Clyde’s hand and he had little choice but to run to keep up with her and Jeremy.

Conner laughed as the rest started to walk along the hallway. “We’ll catch up with them in a few minutes. They’re heading to the recreation dome. It has plenty of vegetation and open areas for sports. We also have two other domes in this cavern for growing food.”

“I assume that you grow your food here in the cavern instead of domes outside due to the radiation?” Alec asked.

“That’s one of the reasons. The severe temperature swings are also a big factor. We’d need to provide lighting regardless since Mars only gets about half of the sunlight that Earth does, so it seemed to make a lot of sense to grow things here.”

As they went through the sliding doors of the recreation area, they found Clyde sitting on a bench inside the doorway and the kids were nowhere in sight.

"You ok?" Lauren asked.

Clyde stood up. "Yeah. Just got a feeling of vertigo for a second there and needed to sit down. I'll be okay."

Lauren's look of concern for Clyde turned to one of shock as she looked beyond him and saw Heather running towards them with an enormous rabbit bounding after her. When Heather reached Lauren, she turned around and put out her hand, offering the carrot that she was carrying. With a final large leap, the rabbit made a perfect landing right in front of her and started to nibble on the carrot.

"My God! That thing is huge! How much does it weight?" Alec asked.

"That's one of the youngsters," Conner said. "I'd guess about fifty pounds or so. Some of the older ones come in closer to one hundred."

"Mom, feel how soft he is," Heather said.

Lauren tentatively reached out to touch the fur, and her hand sunk deep in it.

"It is soft," she said as she started to pet the large animal.

"One of the genetic modifications that we made," Conner said. "In addition to the increase in size, we also gave it angora fur. We used to keep a small dome full of these for both their wool and meat, but since the disaster, we have only kept a few around. Jeremy likes playing with them."

The rabbit had finished the carrot that Heather was holding and was sniffing all over her in hopes of finding another.

The sliding doors opened and Jeremy came in carrying several carrots. "Here you go," Jeremy said as he handed freshly pulled carrots to everyone. "I got these from the crop dome."

As everyone took turns feeding and petting the rabbit, Clyde commented on how tame it was.

"Another little genetic modification—a behavioral one," Conner said. "It involved modifying several genes that we have identified with trust. A big part of aggressive behavior in animals comes through fear. We modified the genes to allow for a much higher degree of trust and hence less fear."

Once the rabbit had ensured that there were no more treats available, it turned and bounded away. The group toured the dome, which looked like it needed a fair bit of upkeep. The grass had not been cut in a long time, lights needed to be replaced, bushes needed pruning, and there were dead plants and leaves all over.

"Since the disaster, the few of us that remain have been overburdened in keeping the essential things running, and this area isn't one of them," Conner said to the unasked question. "Before the disaster, it was heavily used. Soccer was big here then, but we had to use a heavy ball. The trampolines over there were a big hit as well. Nothing like jumping thirty feet in the air!"

After the recreation dome, the group moved over to crop domes, which were in the same state of disrepair as the recreation area.

As the group stepped into the first crop dome, Clyde took a step back. "Whoa!"

"What's wrong," Lauren asked.

"Dudes, I've got the strange feeling that I've been here before. Kind of like a déjà vu moment."

"Well, unless you went sleep walking, that's impossible. You sure you're feeling okay after that dizzy spell?" Lauren said.

Clyde shook his head. "Yeah, I feel fine. It doesn't matter that much; it was just a strange feeling walking in here."

Conner led them through the mostly empty raised growing beds. "For the few of us that remain, we have more than ample stored foods to last until we're all gone," he said. "We only grow enough now for some fresh vegetables."

The reality of the dire situation that faced Conner and the others extinguished the jovial mood that the group had after seeing the rabbits and the recreation area.

After a prolonged pause in the conversation, Clyde seemed to wake up and look around. "Hey, I haven't seen any happy plants around here."

"Happy plants?" Conner asked.

"You know, marijuana plants."

"We don't have any of that here. The best we've been able to do for a recreation product is moonshine."

"Well, today is your lucky day," Clyde said. "I happened to bring along a good supply of seeds from my best strains. When we unload the *Serene Trip*, I'll get them to you and show you the finer points of growing."

Conner grinned. "Well I wasn't planning on getting the supplies from your ship for a few days, but maybe we should make a trip over there today."

"Talking about supplies reminds me," Alec said. "Robert asked me to get a sample of that micro-organism. He thinks it may be of some use on Earth with its appetite for carbon."

"Well, you'll be here about two months before your return flight window opens. I'll arrange to get you a sample before you leave. Maybe some good can come out of its discovery after all.”

“During our time here, I’d also like to go over your notes for your *Hell Turned Ego* cure,” Lauren said.

“Of course; I’ll spend some time with you on that and make sure that you have samples.”

Heather pulled on Alec’s arm and when he leaned over, she whispered into his ear.

Alec laughed. “I’m not sure about that, sweetie.”

“What did she say?” Lauren asked.

“She wants to know if we could somehow bring a pair of the giant bunnies back to Earth.”

“That’ll be tough,” Conner said while looking at Heather. “They’re so used to Martian gravity that they would probably not be able to handle living on Earth.”

Heather nodded with a small pout on her face.

Conner could see the disappointment on her face and thought for a moment. “However, I may be able to make a slight modification to the drugs that I’m giving to Jeremy and have a pair of baby bunnies for you to take a long.”

Heather’s face lit up. “Baby bunnies! They’d be so cute.”

“What about the rule in Percipience about no livestock?” Lauren asked Alec. “Do you think Robert would let her have them?”

“I’d let them run loose,” Alec said. “Robert keeps saying we don’t have enough bio-diversity, and I’m pretty sure with the hind feet these things have that they can protect themselves pretty well.”

"Yeah, you're probably right," Lauren said. "So I guess it would be ok as long as I don't have to clean up the rabbit poop during the flight home."

20 RETURN

The small plane landed on the calm waters by Port Aspire and floated towards the dock. Jake was the first one out followed by the pilot. Jake handed him twenty crisp new YAWNS. "Now remember, if the DC commander asks, you didn't have any passengers on this trip. I'll give you another twenty in a week if I don't hear from him." Despite his best efforts over the last six months, Jake had been unable to convince Erin to stop the attack on Port Aspire or to make an official trip to the village. With the launch less than a week away, all he could now do was warn his son and pray for the best.

"No problem," the pilot said as he smoothly tucked the bills into his pocket. "Nobody is going to ask about this trip. It's a scheduled run that we do every week to bring some supplies for our computer team. But if anyone asks, I'll say that I came up here by myself."

"Thanks," Jake said and then walked up the dock. "Not too much security here," he said as he looked across the beach and saw only groups of kids playing on the rocks and more playing on some contraption made up of tubes, slides, and running water. He walked up a well-worn path towards a large structure. Entering the building, he was greeted by a young man.

"Where can I find Alec?" Jake asked.

"He's not here; he's been gone for a long time. You're in luck though; he radioed in a little while ago and will be attempting a landing tomorrow."

"Landing? Attempting? Where's he coming from?"

"Don't you know? Mars, of course!"

"Mars!" Jake said unbelievably.

"You must be from Epoch or Provenance. Why don't you discuss this with our leader, Robert. He left here a little while ago and is going to take the *Fly About Thing* to meet Alec."

Jake did not even bother asking what the *Fly About Thing* was and simply asked for directions to find Robert and left with a brisk pace.

Jake's eyes grew wide as he cleared the forest and saw the airship on the other side of the hemp field. He quickened his pace and reached the large airship as Robert was untying the last of the retaining ropes.

"What are you doing here?" Robert asked, not holding back his displeasure as he looked down at Jake.

"Where's Alec and what's this I hear about Mars?"

"It'll take too long for me to explain. Now what are you doing here?"

"I came to warn you. Erin is planning on sending missiles towards Port Aspire very soon."

"Like I'm going to trust you. You and Erin were the ones that initiated that radiation cloud over Percipience!"

"It wasn't me! I found out through Erin that it was Jordan who masterminded that. You've got to believe that I knew nothing about it."

"Jordan? Why would he do that?"

"I'm guessing that he wasn't too impressed with the setback you gave us ten years ago. I actually told him to not do anything against Percipience, but I imagine he thought that he'd impress me and go ahead anyhow. Now what's this I'm hearing about my son and Mars?"

"I don't have time to explain. I'm on a tight schedule and need to get to where Alec is going to land. Come along and I'll explain on the way."

****

The two months that the team spent at Noria waiting for their return flight window went by quickly. The first few weeks were consumed with unloading the cargo from the *Serene Trip* and then replenishing her with fuel, oxygen, and other key items needed for the return trip to Earth.

Conner and the other few remaining Norians were like kids at Christmas time as they opened the cargo containers. Much of the cargo was comprised of tools, parts, lab equipment, and medicine that were difficult or impossible to build on Mars. These were all greatly appreciated, but the real excitement came over the non-essential items.

One of the crates contained a variety of hibernating caterpillars, which they placed in the recreation dome, the perfect location for when they transformed into butterflies. Other crates contained printed fiction books and an assortment of things that could survive the eight-month journey, including fish and bumble bees for honey.

Heather and Jeremy were inseparable and spent nearly the entire time in the recreation dome while Lauren spent her time in Conner's lab on a crash course in understanding the *Hell Turning Ego* cure.

Alec and Clyde helped in the crop domes, planting both Clyde's special seeds plus some from the seed bank. With some parts they brought from Earth, they also repaired the video feed between Earth and Mars and took several tours with Conner on the Martian surface to obtain soil samples for Robert.

When it was finally time for the return trip, Jeremy was stressed and sad at leaving Conner until he was reminded by Alec that they were going to try and make at least one more trip; if they did, he could come along. He also reminded Jeremy that with the video link fixed, he could see Conner anytime that he wanted to.

****

The Earth loomed large through the front window of the cockpit. "Well, I guess it's time to punch in the landing location," Alec said to Clyde who was sitting beside him in the co-pilot seat.

With a few keystrokes, Alec brought up the menu of pre-programmed landing locations and selected the Area-51 site. Within seconds, a green light lit up on the control panel indicating that the landing beacons were acquired.

"Looks like Robert did his part by turning on those beacons," Clyde said while they waited for the computer to finish loading the site specific landing information. There was a loud beep and a message came up on a display. Instead of the standard "Program loaded" message, "Load error" appeared.

The men looked at each other. "What's that about?" Alec said tensely.

"Not sure. Try it again."

Alec repeated the procedure two more times with the same results.

"Manual landing?" Clyde asked.

"I don't see how we have much choice," Alec said as his palms started to sweat. "We'll only get one shot at it too. Though this takes off and lands like a plane, I'm sure we won't have enough fuel to circle around if we abort the first attempt."

Clyde informed the others of the problem and warned them to buckle in tight as it may be a rough landing. Jeremy and Heather took her bunnies out of their cage, wrapped them in blankets, and put them in Jeremy's pack. Clyde returned to the cockpit and pulled out the detailed information needed for the landing so that he could assist Alec.

The initial entry went smooth and the spaceplane stayed in the flightpath with only the occasional warning going off, which Alec or Clyde quickly corrected for. The ship started to shake more than normal as they entered the upper atmosphere and Alec had his hands full in keeping it on the intended course of going through a series of wide-banked turns to slow down their speed.

"So far you're looking not too bad," Clyde said in an attempt to raise Alec's confidence. There were several warnings coming up on the console and the occasional alarm bell but nothing critical. That is until they got to the final approach.

"You're coming in too shallow," Clyde yelled over the increasing number of alarms.

"I know," Alec said. "It's not responding like the flight simulator."

Alec fought to bring the craft to a better position as they were close enough to see the runway and the airship close by it.

"My God! He's coming in pretty fast and low. Is that normal?" Jake said to Robert.

"I don't know. I've never seen a landing before."

The two men watched as the spaceplane hit the runway and then bounced back up in the air. The second time it hit the runway the craft was not angled straight causing the front landing gear to snap off and the front of the craft to hit the ground. With the nose digging into the hard clay, the craft started to spin violently off of the runway area and then flipped over twice before coming to a stop.

The men ran towards the crash site. When they arrived, there was smoke coming from the craft and Robert could see flames around the fuel tank. Thankfully, the craft ended up right side up and without any front landing gear, it was low enough for the two men to reach the entry hatch underneath it. With some effort, they managed to open it and they went inside.

The light from the hatchway revealed smoke inside the cabin area and coughing could be heard from the back. Robert and Jake headed towards the rear seating area and started to unbuckle people and drag them out of the hatch. There were groans from some and no life signs at all from others as they pulled or carried them to a safe distance from the crash site. Robert went back inside, noticing that the smoke was getting thicker. He searched and found no one left in the cabin area so he headed to the cockpit.

He found Clyde wincing in pain as he was trying to unbuckle himself.

"You okay?" Robert asked.

"My arm is broken for sure. Help me unbuckle this damn thing."

Robert undid the buckle and then looked over to the pilot seat and immediately knew by the angle of his head that Alec did not make it. Not letting his emotions take over, Robert picked up Clyde and took him out to the others and then went back to retrieve Alec's body and noticed that the flames were getting bigger and the smoke thicker. With a large breath, he entered the craft one more time and came out quickly carrying Alec. By the time he had reached the safe area, the craft was fully engulfed in flames.

When she returned to consciousness, Lauren knew immediately that something was wrong. "Alec!" she cried as she could no longer sense his presence. Robert quickly came over and knelt on the sand beside her. "He didn't make it."

"The others?"

"Everyone else is alive. Banged up and a few broken bones, especially Clyde. But I think they're going to make it."

Heather limped over to her mom and Grandpa with tears in her eyes.

"Are you okay, honey?" Lauren asked.

"I'm fine. But Daddy!"

"I know," Lauren said as she hugged her daughter.

For the first time in his adult life, Jake wept as he knelt by Alec as he thought of the good times they had together and deeply regretted the separation they had over the last decade.

The loud explosion of one of the fuel tanks brought Jake and Robert out of their grieving for a moment. They stood up and looked at each other.

"The attack on Port Aspire is imminent," Jake said. "Probably within the next day."

"Not enough time to evacuate," Robert replied. "I guess we could fly over to Epoch and Lauren could extend the Hive over your city."

"That won't work. Erin has thought of that and has constant air patrols around Epoch. You won't be able to get within a hundred miles of Epoch without being spotted and shot down."

Robert shook his head. "It'll take a day just to get to Port Aspire from here. All we can do is contact them via radio to warn them. It won't help much but maybe some people can get away." He then looked over to Alec's body. "Percipience, Noria, and now Port Aspire. Everything is lost for our society."

Jake thought for a while. "That new drug that you told me about may have worked. I don't' agree with your way of life, but perhaps there is some common ground and our two cultures could have co-existed. But that's all a moot point now. You don't have the drug and even if you did, there isn't enough time to let it take effect."

They heard a cough behind them as Clyde cleared his throat. He had lifted himself up into a sitting position. "The instructions for creating the drug were in there," he said pointing with his one good arm towards the nearby fire. All that's left is this one sample that he gave us." Clyde reached into his front pocket and pulled out a vial. "But like you said, even if we could make more, there's no time to get the drug to Provenance and have it take effect."

Heather was paying attention to the conversation while being cradled and rocked by Lauren. "Why don't we have time, Grandpa?"

Robert attempted to dismiss Heather's comment. "Don't worry about it, sweetie."

"Jeremy and I can give the people at Provenance and Epoch the stuff that his dad made."

"Sweetie, we need to have given it to them years ago. Giving it to them now will do no good."

"We can do that."

"Do what?"

"I could go back in time and give it to them," Heather said.

All eyes were now on Heather. Jeremy got up with some effort and stood beside her, nodding his head.

"Excuse us for a moment," Lauren said. "I need to have a conversation with these two."

The telepathic exchange took less than a minute; Lauren stood up and looked towards the other adults. "Well, it seems that they can do this," Lauren said. "I've always expected that it was possible and these two, with their strong psychic skills, have figured it out."

"This is ludicrous!" Jake exclaimed. "We need to be starting the evacuation at Port Aspire not this hocus pocus stuff."

Robert ignored Jake's outburst. "Can you explain to me how it works?"

"I can try," Lauren said. "Time is kind of like any other physical dimension. For the physical ones, we can look and see what's here and also what's ten feet away. Well time works in the same way. If you could stand back and look across the time dimension, you could see the events that happened a long time ago—the current events and the future events all, pardon the pun, at the same time."

"Okay, I understand what you're saying. Not believing it, but understanding." Robert said.

"Well, if you have strong enough psychic abilities, then you can will yourself to another point in time. I've always suspected that it was possible, especially with my meditation sessions near the pyramid where there's a convergence of ley lines. These two have stronger physic powers than me by far and they've found something that allows them to focus these powers."

"What?" Robert asked.

Jeremy reached into his pocket and opened the cloth. "With the glowing artifacts that Heather showed me," Jeremy said. "It took us all of the first night that Heather arrived at Noria, but we finally figured out what they are and how they work."

"We can do it, Grandpa!" Heather said. "We already did it once to Clyde."

"What? I don't remember anything of that," Clyde said.

"Yes you do," Jeremy said. "That vertigo you felt when entering the recreation area in Noria and then the déjà vu you encountered when visiting the crop domes."

Jake looked at Clyde. "Are you buying any of this?"

"Well, I do remember the weird déjà vu experience in the crop dome. That really freaked me out. But what about all of the paradoxes that go with time travel. Like if I go back and kill my dad before I'm born. Do I disappear too?"

"No, you'd still exist," Lauren said. "If I travel to another point in time and do something, anything, then this will immediately alter all of the future. If you go back and kill your parents before you're born, you exist in that moment of time but not in the future. No paradox."

"OK, I don't kill my parents, but I alter something in the past. When I come back to the present, how's that reconciled in my memories? I'll have the original set of memories from before I travelled and then will I also have a different set of memories based on what I changed?"

"Okay, in time travel, if you go to a time where you're already there physically, then you'll merge with the mind of that body. It may take your mind some time to sort things out, but you'll retain both sets of memories as best as your mind can handle. This also applies when returning, since after all it is just another time jump. If you go to a time where you're not physically there, then a new you is created in that time at a location that you can control and the original you disappears. Mass is always conserved."

"Ah, that helps explains some of the cases reported over the centuries of pre-cognition or déjà vu where people can vividly recall historical events or foretell what will happen in the future."

"Exactly."

"What if I go to a time that's a year before I'm conceived?"

Lauren laughed. "Then you're in trouble. Similar to when you suddenly appeared when you time shifted to a year before your birth, you'll disappear as soon as you're conceived. All of the other rules apply and since at conception you're unable to understand all of your memories, they'll be lost. Basically you'll disappear without a trace and be replaced by the newly conceived you."

"Ok, note to self: Do not do that! But I could keep time travelling back to a younger me and live forever, right?"

"Well sort of, but remember when time shifting to a time when you exist, your mind does the reconciliation of the two different sets of memories. If you're fifty and travel back to when you're twenty-five, your mind will lose a lot of the memories you had when you were fifty. In fact, when it is over, you probably won't have remembered time shifting at all."

"Look, this is all crazy," Jake said. "Even if we could do this, sending these two kids back isn't going to help us too much since they don't understand the science or what really needs to be done. Can we please get off of this silly topic and warn Port Aspire?"

"You're underestimating them," Lauren said. "When time travelling, they can travel themselves and take others with them. That's as long as they have a strong connection with the conscious of the other people, like through physical contact. So, several of us can go back, including me. I spent a fair bit of time with Conner and his cure. I could resynthesize it."

"Jake, I know you don't believe in all of this and quite frankly I'm having a hard time as well," Robert said. "But I have complete belief in Lauren, and if she says that the kids can do it, then I say we go for it, but we need to get back to the area around Percipience. If this time travel does work, then who knows what will be in this space if we change things. The only area that we know has been constant for the last few hundred years is the Wildlife Preserve that Richard setup around Percipience. And yes, as soon as we get back to the airship, I'll send a message to Port Aspire."

"You still trying to figure this out?" Lauren asked Clyde who was staring off into space.

"I'm not even trying to," Clyde said. "What I was thinking though was why go back and use the drug at Provenance. Why not go back to right before the Great Loss and change the virus that caused it, Virtuesh-B. Instead of making it a lethal virus, we could make it to be the carrier of this new cure that Conner developed. Also, if we could put it in the very first batch, then we won't need much of Conner's drug."

"Holy crap! That's a great idea. We'd have to go back to the place where it was made though, and there's no exact reference to that in Richard's diary," Robert said.

"Well, we'll have to go back and find Richard then!" Clyde said.

The time travel conversation was a good distraction, but as they started to move to the airship, the events of the past few hours sunk back in. It was specifically brought home as Robert carried Alec's lifeless body up the ramp of the airship and placed it gently on the floor in the cabin.

"We'll have a proper funeral for him when we get back," Robert said as he put his arms around Lauren to comfort her. He then covered the body with a blanket and headed up to the cockpit to radio Port Aspire and then pilot the ship to Bear Lake.

The trip was quiet with everyone lost in their own thoughts about the disaster that had occurred at Area-51 or the impending doom for Port Aspire. Robert pushed his emotions aside and busied himself by borrowing Richard's journal from Clyde and making notes on several pieces of paper, which he then rolled up into two separate rolls and put into his shirt pocket.

Robert landed the airship close to the old shoreline of Bear Lake and then, with the pyramid in the background and with Jake and Clyde watching, Lauren, Robert, Heather, and Jeremy formed a meditation circle near the old lake shoreline.

****

"The missiles are on course and should reach their destination within the hour," the private reported out loud.

"Excellent," Erin said. "Have you heard back from our guards over in Epoch?"

"Yes, but still no sighting of Jake."

"The fool. I bet he went up to Port Aspire to warn them. That's too bad; I was starting to like him too."

21 HOPEFUL

Robert was doing his best to regulate his breathing and to bring his mind into focus; he then had an incredible sense of vertigo. He opened his eyes and everything looked the same but different as well. It was cooler and the trees seemed to have shifted, either being smaller, taller, or in different places. He noticed that the others were also looking around too. He then looked behind him and was shocked to see that the pyramid had disappeared and that the water from the lake was close to them.

"It worked!" Lauren said. "Heather has brought us back to the day before Percipience's chief scientist, Olivia, returns with samples of the Virtuesh-B virus. We should be able to get over to Percipience in time to meet her and get the details we need about the Asia lab that made both the original Virtuesh and airborne Virtuesh-B virus in the first place."

Though he tried to keep up during the hike back to Percipience, Jeremy could not. He could walk in the higher gravity of Earth, but he tired quickly. But this was only partially the reason. The other was the newness of everything he encountered and the constant barrage of questions that he asked. Eventually, Robert offered to carry him on his shoulders.

As they approached Percipience, they all were shocked at the differences. Everything was so new and there was construction and heavy equipment everywhere. *No wonder it was taking so long to build up Port Aspire*, Robert thought to himself as they slipped around the security and hid amongst the rows of temporary trailers.

With everyone out working, the trailer area was, allowing them time to look through several of them to find spare pale orange overalls for everyone, except for Robert who had to do with the largest size that he could find, which was still much too short in both the legs and arms. With their disguises complete, they headed towards the brand new town hall and specifically to the Research Lab. Robert let Lauren, Jeremy and Heather go into the lab by themselves while he took a quick tour of the newly built facilities.

Upon entering the lab, Lauren found a young women working at one of the lab benches.

"Olivia?" Lauren asked.

"Yes, who are you? I haven't seen you before," Olivia said

Lauren noticed the vials that Olivia was handling and made sure to keep her distance. "What should be an easy answer, I'm afraid is not. Perhaps you should sit down as I explain."

Over the next hour, Lauren explained to Olivia exactly who she was and what she was hoping to accomplish. At the end, Olivia looked at her and said, "So, let me see if I have this straight. There are four of you from about two hundred years in the future and you've travelled back in time to see me. You want to find out where the Virtuesh virus is made and then you're going to modify it so that it's no longer lethal but instead will cause a behavioral change in people."

"I know it sounds far-fetched—" Lauren started to say but was interrupted as Robert entered the lab. "This is my father, Robert. Dad, I 've just finished explaining to Olivia why we're here."

Olivia was taken back by the size of Robert. "This is far beyond far-fetched. Ludicrous is more like it. What kind of fool do you take me for? Is this some kind of joke or test by the Pleasant Belief Foundation? I'm going to call security."

At that moment, Olivia started to rise from her seat and not by her own power—she started floating. Lauren took a quick look at Heather who was staring intently at Olivia. "Heather, put her down!"

Olivia gently floated back in her seat and was visibly shaken by what had happened.

"I know that we can't prove everything that we've said, but that little demonstration from my daughter should be enough for you to at least to consider that what we're telling you is the truth."

"Even if this were all true, how could you modify the Virtuesh virus? None of you have any experience with it. I'm one of the few people on the planet that does. You'd need me to help you break into the Asian lab and do that work all without being detected. How on earth would we do that?"

"I may be able to help there," came a deep voice from the back of the room. It was a young delivery man who had come in unnoticed.

Everyone turned to the young man. "Who are you and how long have you been here?" Robert asked.

"My name is Hope and long enough to hear this wild plan plus see that little demonstration. Forgive the disguise but I've been working for Mikhail on gathering intelligence on what Olivia has been up to." The more that Hope spoke, the higher the pitch of her voice went as the Xeon gas started to wear off. She started to remove her disguise.

"Hope! It is you! How could you help with this wild plan?" Olivia asked.

"Let's just say that I have many talents and I'm pretty sure that you'll need several of them if you want to pull this off. I think that Mikhail is out of control and quite frankly I'm scared to death of his plan. I haven't been able to think of a way to stop him, even by getting Richard involved. Since the Virtuesh-B virus is already made and distributed to the people that are going to release it, it's unstoppable. This all sounds pretty wild but if what these strangers are saying is true, then there's an outside chance that it could work."

After a quick group discussion, a modified plan was built up. Hope, Lauren, and Olivia would time travel back with the assistance of Jeremy about two years to when Virtuesh-B was first developed and modify the virus at this point.

"How long are you going to need for your work?" Hope asked Olivia.

"It'll take a while. I understand the Virtuesh-B virus really well, but integrating this new genetic stuff from them, even with Lauren's help, will take several days. I need to design the whole thing so that Virtuesh-B is still lethal for at least a few weeks so that it can pass its tests, all the while hide the new stuff so that it isn't detected."

"Okay, sounds like a tough job but can it be done in three days?"

"Maybe."

"Jeremy, I'm not sure how precise you can be, but ideally we want to be at the lab right before a long weekend. If I can get us in, that should give us three uninterrupted days to work."

"I shouldn't have any problem putting us exactly when and where you want," Jeremy replied.

Lauren, Hope, and Olivia headed back to the trailers to get ready and agreed to meet Robert, Jeremy, and Heather back at the Research Lab in one hour. Without knowing exactly what they were going to run into at the Asia facility, Hope packed a backpack with disguises and tools. The three young women then discarded their overalls for civilian clothes and returned to the lab.

"I've been thinking about this plan," Robert said when they arrived. "If it succeeds, then it's critical that both Olivia and Hope not interfere with the activities that are going to transpire here over the next weeks. We need to ensure that Virtuesh-B is released."

"That includes the attempt that Hope is going to make tonight to kill Olivia and Diane," Lauren said. "From what I've read in Richard's journal, that's a critical part of the near future and is the catalyst to get things moving."

"You're planning on killing me and Diane?"

Hope put on a fake innocent look. "Sorry, that's the plan. But that also confirms that Lauren is from the future since nobody knows about that plan besides Mikhail and me."

Lauren could see the look of stress on Olivia's face. "Don't worry, Hope doesn't succeed. Oh, by the way. Hope, don't take any of the Virtuesh-B vaccine from this lab. Olivia has coated them with the original Virtuesh virus. I think you should lay low for a few weeks."

Hope looked at Olivia. "You were going to try and kill me?"

"Sorry," Olivia said as she mimicked Hope's earlier fake innocent look.

The three young women and Jeremy then sat down on the floor in one of the lecture halls and held hands to form a meditation circle. Jeremy gave one of the cubes to Heather. "In case we don't make it back," he said to her while giving her a hug.

Robert and Heather watched and soon they were alone in the room.

"Grandpa has a special mission for you," Robert said to Heather, "but we must be quick."

****

The sense of vertigo was less this time for Lauren, and she quickly recovered to find her and the others in a park in the middle of the night.

They rented a room in a nearby hotel, bought enough prepared food to last four days, and then Lauren, Jeremy, and Olivia slept while Hope did a reconnaissance trip to the Asia Lab. She returned later in the afternoon.

"Well, I think we're set," Hope said. "There are a lot of people leaving the lab early today since the long weekend starts tomorrow and I think that I've figured out a way for us to get in."

"How?"

"Surprisingly, the security at the facility is light. There are several places on the outside that aren't even covered by cameras. So I think the best way for us to get in is to simply cut a hole in the security fence in one of these uncovered spots and then go through one of the employee entrances. I've rigged up a little diversion on the other side of the building that I'll set off with my phone when we're ready."

At dusk, they left the hotel and went over to the lab. Hiding out in a ditch near the fence, Hope took out her phone and entered in a special key sequence. Immediately, they could hear several car alarms go off in the distance, and they saw most of the guards at the gate head out to investigate the source of the noise.

Making short work of cutting a hole in the fence and bypassing the electronic lock on the employee entrance, Hope led the team into the building. The place was deserted due to the upcoming long weekend; Hope had everyone stay in one of the washrooms while she did a quick look around. When she returned, she had a big grin on her face.

"What are you so happy about?" Olivia asked.

"Sometimes a plan comes together better than it really should," Hope replied. "I was on the floor directly above us and noticed a female security guard entering a washroom. So I followed her in and was able to scan her RFID chip from her badge with my phone without her even noticing. This should give us access to any room in the place. I think that your virus is in a lab on that floor as well since there's a fair bit more protective gear and fancier labs."

"Probably a biohazard level four area," Olivia said. "Lead the way."

They took the stairs to the next floor and found the lab that Hope had referred to.

"This has to be the place," Olivia said. "This is the only lab that we have seen that has the protection necessary for such a dangerous virus."

Hope used her phone to gain access; the team followed her into the lab. While they went to work, she disabled the motion sensors in the room and then pretended to key herself out. "The computer will now think that this room is empty and won't trip an alarm if the security guard, whose ID we're using, starts to open doors in other sections of the building."

The team then settled in with Hope and Jeremy taking turns sleeping and keeping watch while Lauren and Olivia did their biological magic.

On the third afternoon, a bleary-eyed Olivia looked up from examining the most recent test results. "Got it!" she said. "I can't test it fully, but it looks like it should work perfectly. I've set this up on their master copy of Virtuesh-B as well, which will be used to clone the rest of the virus."

"Great, now let's get out of here," Hope said.

"No need," Jeremy said. "We can get back right from here."

"Duh, of course!" Hope said. "I didn't think of that."

After making sure they had left no signs of their stay, the three women and young boy sat on the floor and held hands.

It had only been a few minutes since the trio of women and Jeremy had left Robert and Heather when all of a sudden they re-appeared.

The now familiar vertigo wore off quickly and Lauren gave both her daughter and dad big hugs. "It worked! Olivia and I were able to modify Virtuesh-B."

"Okay, well our job here is done then. It's time for us to head back," Robert said. He then reached into his pocket and pulled out one of the two rolled up paper notes and gave it to Olivia. "Olivia, in the not too distant future, if things go to plan, you'll find yourself with Richard in Diane's RV heading back to Percipience. At that time, please give him this note.

"What's on it?"

"Changing people's behavior isn't enough to save this planet. Something else needs to be done as well and this note outlines the details. Richard is the only person on the planet that I know that can do this, so it's important that he gets it."

Olivia took the note. "Okay, I'll do my best."

After goodbyes and hugs were exchanged, Robert, Lauren, Jeremy, and Heather sat down on the floor and formed the meditation circle and vanished from the room.

****

It took several hours to reach his lawyer and arrive at agreement on the wording of the pardon to his satisfaction. The others watched tensely through the two-way mirror as Richard re-entered the interrogation room.

Diane felt the bulk of her revolver under her coat; an inner rage built within her. *He's going to get away with killing hundreds of people, including my brother.*

Olivia felt mentally exhausted. The last few weeks had frayed her nerves, first with the visit from the group from the future and then acting as if nothing had happened while watching Mikhail follow through with his plan. She was nervous too; her work at the Asia lab and integrating the behavior-modifying drug with the virus had been rushed and she really could not test it very well. If this was the case, she feared that the Virtuesh-B that was out there may still be lethal. She moved closer to Spencer for support, but he wanted nothing to do with her and seem mesmerized by the scene unfolding on the other side of the mirror.

Sue was glad it would be soon over. She glanced down at her vibrating phone and saw the DIR security team number displayed. Not wanting to miss the interaction between Richard and Mikhail, she ignored the call.

"The deal is in place, Mikhail. What more do you need to call off the release? I don't want you to just postpone it for two days. The agreement is to call it off completely. It isn't stated directly in the agreement, but I'm telling you now that none of your family or friends will be released until all the virus cylinders are returned and accounted for."

Mikhail pointed to the computer that still showed his family and friends bound to chairs. "I assumed as much. I'll enter the code to have my people return the virus. By the way, my compliments on adding something for yourself in the agreement by negotiating to keep your villages safe. Nice touch."

"Yes, I thought so too," Richard said. He unbound Mikhail and followed behind him as he moved towards the computer. As he placed his hands over the keyboard, the two-way mirror shattered. Three gunshots exploded in quick succession. Mikhail slumped to the floor with the bullet holes in a tight pattern on his chest. Bright red blood spread across his shirt and quickly started to form a pool on the floor. In the seconds it took for everyone to understand what had happened, Spencer had placed his gun on the floor, raised his arms, and put his hands behind his head.

Richard bent over Mikhail's slumped body and could see that he was dead. He looked up through the broken mirror and shook his head.

"Spencer! What have you done?" Sue screamed.

"My job," he said. Two soldiers entered the interrogation room and fixed their weapons on him through the splintered mirror.

"Are you crazy?"

He brushed his hand across his face. "It was almost comical listening to you brag about the spies you had all over the world when I first came on board. My loyalties are to a small Asian nation. The ruler is tired of Western corruption and politics and attempts on his life. I knew I had discovered the answer for him in the virus and vaccine. When I gave you the samples, I had already sent the same to him. My entire country has been vaccinated against the virus during the last few months."

"You're a traitor!"

"Only from your perspective. In my country, I'm a hero."

On the trip back to Percipience in Diane's RV, Olivia saw Richard head to the back and reach for his cell phone. She got up and headed towards him, reached into her bag, pulled out a roll of paper, and gave it to him.

"What's this?" Richard asked.

"You wouldn't believe me if I told you," Olivia replied. "But you must trust me that it's genuine and a great deal of effort was made to get it to you at this moment."

22 BACK TO THE FUTURE

LA Times March 29, 2236

The national twenty-four hour work week law has passed its second vote today and is expected to pass the third and final vote next week. When implemented, it will replace the current thirty-two hour work week standard that has been in effect for over one hundred years. The new four-day weekend will not come soon enough for many citizens who have lobbied for it for decades.

In other news, it was announced today that for the first time in two hundred years, the average global greenhouse gas levels have dropped below 400 ppm. "This is a significant milestone that every person on the planet can take pride in," the president was quoted as saying. Through a combination of drastically reduced consumption, lower population, and the efforts of the Pleasant Belief Foundation in removing carbon dioxide from the atmosphere, we've managed to turn the tide on what could have been a planet-wide disaster."

It is expected that our president will meet next month with other world leaders who are also mostly affiliated with the CURE party to start the formation of a single worldwide government. The president was quoted as saying, "The role of government has changed over the last few hundred years from one of promoting growth to one of facilitating the coordination of people. This will be better done if we are dealing with a single organization."

****

Robert felt the vertigo feeling slowly going away. When he opened his eyes, he found that he was on a bed in the nursing station at Percipience.

"There you are!" said a familiar person standing next to him who he could not quite put a name on as his mind tried to get a grasp on reality. "I was starting to get worried about you and the others who the nurse said passed out all at the same time."

"How long have I been out?"

"I'm told nearly a day. I just got back to Percipience myself and am completely confused. There are people here and no radiation. I'm glad that you're ok so we can try to figure out what happened. How are you feeling?"

"I'm not sure." Robert closed his eyes and tried to recall what happened. He remembered teaching some kids in his lab and then all of a sudden feeling light-headed. After that, nothing. Then there was another memory that started to come into focus. One which seemed like a different life but he knew it was his. In this memory, there was a great deal of conflict with other villages, pollution, a giant airship, Mars, and then the death of his son-in-law, Alec.

"Who are…" Robert started to ask but was interrupted by a groan coming from the bed next to his.

"Ah, Lauren!" the attendant said. "Glad you decided to join us in the world of the living. You're the last one to recover. I was told that Heather woke up hours ago, but I haven't been able to find her."

"Alec!" Lauren cried out as she struggled to get out of bed to hold him. "You're alive? How can this be?" Tears of joy poured from her face as she finally managed to get her arms around him.

"Yes, of course. When was I supposed to have died?"

Lauren looked over to her father who was still lying in bed and saw a huge smile start to form on his face as his memories started to become clearer.

"What happened?" she demanded from him. "He died! I was there when it happened!"

"Are you sure you're ok?" Alec asked. "I think I would've remember if I died."

"Well, I was not sure it would all work out, but it looks like it did," Robert said. "During our time travel back, when you, Heather, and Jeremy went to talk to Olivia, I went over to the office area and found a phone. I had written down Richard's cell phone number that was in his journal and gave him a call."

"You did what?" Alec asked as he tried to keep up with a conversation that made no sense at all to him.

"I called him and I was amazed when he picked up. I then told him that he really needed to do one thing and that was to put a second backup landing configuration for the Area-51 runway into the proto-type spaceship. As soon as I did this, I believe that the subsequent time immediately took this into account. This means that when the first configuration failed to load for Alec when he was approaching Earth, he could use the backup one and land perfectly."

"Okay, that I remember," Alec said. "I was panicked when we got the load error on the first attempt and was relieved that there was a second backup configuration to try."

"But…" Lauren started to say.

"Let me finish; there's more. So I also knew that as soon as Olivia had figured out how to put the new drug into the Virtuesh-B virus, the future time events would change again and most likely would cause Alec to have never been, since Epoch would not have formed. So, as soon as you, Olivia, and Jeremy time shifted to go to the Asia Lab, I had Heather go and pickup Alec, Clyde, and Jake and move them a single day into the future. Then when Olivia worked her magic, the whole timeline changed and the Great Loss never happened. Since Alec, Clyde and Jake had shifted in time, they were still here after the dust settled."

"OK, in some twisted way, this is starting to make sense," Alec said. "After the landing from Mars, we went to the pyramids and then you two, Jeremy, and Heather went back into time. Heather came back on her own and then left again. Jake, Clyde and I waited overnight for you to return. When we awoke the next morning, you hadn't returned and the *Fly About Thing* was gone, so we decided to walk back to Port Aspire. When Heather came back, she must have shifted us that one day."

Just then Heather burst into the nursing station with two large white rabbits hopping closely by her side. "Grandpa! You're awake!"

"You bet, sweetie. Why are you in such good mood?"

"I've been talking to Jeremy. He's back on Mars and said to thank you."

Robert smiled and turned towards Lauren. "The other little thing I told Richard was to pass a warning on to Noria about the carbon-eating microorganism."

"What was on that roll of paper that you gave to Olivia to give to Richard?" Lauren asked.

"A note telling him that he had to do more on reducing overall carbon in both the air and water. I suggested that he put Percipience in charge of monitoring this. I'm still trying to sort out both of these memory lines, but I think it worked too since the CO2 level is now about three-quarters what it was back in 2022."

Lauren closed her eyes and tried to clear the cobwebs out. "Ah, I'm starting to remember now. The *Hell Turned Ego* cure seems to have worked as well. The world population is decreasing and resource consumption is way down."

"I've no idea what both of you are talking about; I have a lot of catching up to do. I don't know anything about this timeline," Alec said. "Plus I need to build a new airship!"

Clyde and Jake entered the nursing station. "OK, dude," Clyde said while looking at Alec. "Things are seriously messed up. Besides people living in Percipience again, no one has even heard of Port Aspire. Then the really strange thing is that even though I knew everyone I ran into, nobody knew who I was."

"Makes sense," Robert said. "With GDP and complete isolation from the rest of the world, things would turn out pretty much the same way as they did in the old timeline."

"What?" Clyde asked.

Alec pulled his dad and Clyde aside and did his best to explain the events that had happened.

All of a sudden, Lauren became very solemn.

"What's wrong?" Her dad asked.

"Logan and Lucas! I just realized that in this timeline they don't exist since Alec and I've never met until now."

Heather giggled.

"Heather! This isn't something to laugh about," Lauren scolded.

"Sorry, Mommy. But I was wondering the same thing this morning and had a feeling. So I time travelled a few years into the future. I'm going to be their big sister!"

Lauren nodded as she tried to get a handle on her feelings and walked over to Alec to tell him the news.

"Heather, I don't think you should be travelling about in time without someone with you," Robert said.

"I don't think that I can anymore, Grandpa; both mine and Jeremy's cubes aren't shining very brightly anymore. I think we've used them up or something."

The entire group decided that some sunshine and a meal were needed to help get everyone on the same page with timelines and next steps. Alec led the way as the group headed out of the nursing station to go to Robert's clan hut.

****

Sitting at a picnic table on Windmill Hill and using a set of binoculars, an old man saw the group leave the town center building. He put down the binoculars and jotted some notes down in a well-travelled journal.

March 29, 2236

Though through a path that I'd never would have thought of when I started this quest, somehow everything has worked out. There are so many things that could have gone wrong along the way and so there must be a hand guiding things. Though my years are now numbered, there are a few things that I must finish and will detail them in my next entry in this journal.

Richard then closed the book, picked up the brightly glowing cube sitting beside it and vanished.

Appendices

APPENDIX A – ENTITLEMENT

*"When we replace a sense of service and gratitude with a sense of entitlement and expectation, we quickly see the demise of our relationships, society, and economy.'
— Steve Maraboli, Unapologetically You: Reflections on Life and the Human Experience*

"When we let go of 'stuff,' we discover that the only lasting, dependable security comes from controlling less not more, opening up to life, loosening the rigid boundaries of self, letting other people in, and become tied—that is more dependent, not less—to a community of people and the community of nature." http://www.unique-design.net/library/control.html

Throughout the Percipience series, I've attempted to raise awareness in four areas that I fear are approaching global tipping points. The first three—the environment, natural resource usage, and the economy—were brought up in the first two books. Within this book, the fourth issue is introduced: the deterioration of how we, as individuals, treat each other and how our society functions.

First of all, do we really have an issue here? It is a given that with our ever-increasing knowledge, new technology, and population growth, there will be changes to the way our society works. There will be changes to what we consider morally acceptable and there will be changes to our behavior. The question is: Are some of these changes significant enough to be worthy of concern? Are some of these changes actually pushing us past a tipping point upon where our society can no longer function and ends in social disintegration?

Let's start by looking at some examples of changes that are occurring in our society today:

- Divorce is common place, many of us do not know our neighbors, and many kids seldom stay in touch with parents or grandparents. All types of relationships require sacrifice on both sides, yet many people expect others to sacrifice for them without reciprocating.

- With some exceptions, there is a general decreasing trend for church and community involvement.

- There is an increase use of drugs for mental disorders in both adults and children and an increase use of instant weight loss clinics and plastic surgery.

- Gambling and viewing of online pornography is increasing.

- In many education systems, teachers now need to foster students' self-esteem by either not failing them, always focusing on the good, and giving awards for participation instead of results.

- A majority of the population expects pensions, social security, health care, inheritances, homes, large televisions, and new cars.

- There is an expectation by many to be compensated for any perceived wrongdoing to them

Can you see the common thread in all of these points? The fundamental change that is occurring right now in our society is that the needs of ourselves are becoming more important than the needs of others. We are becoming less grateful for what we have. We feel like we deserve more. We feel like we are **entitled** to things without having to put in the effort to earn them.

This feeling of entitlement also explains our excessive resource usage and our basic disregard for polluting the planet and for running up sky-high government debts for our children to pay off. There is little caring of how we impact others, and the only thing that is important is that we get what we want and that we get it right now.

There is a common thread that runs across most religions and is also one that I believe most people without religious affiliations believe in. This thread is called the Golden Rule or the ethic of reciprocity. Here are some examples:

The Hindu Golden Rule:

"One should never do that to another which one regards as injurious to one's own self."
-- Brihaspati, Mahabharata (Anusasana Parva, Section CXIII, Verse 8)
[Hindu Teaching ~3200 BC]

The Jewish Golden Rule:

"That which is hateful to you, do not do to your fellow."
-- Talmud, Shabbat 31a, the "Great Principle"

The Confucian Golden Rule:

"Never impose on others what you'd not choose for yourself."
-- Confucius ~500 BC Chinese Philosopher (Analects XV.24)

The Christian Golden Rule:

"Do unto others as you'd have them do unto you."
-- Jesus ~30 AD [Luke 6:31]

The Islam Golden Rule:

"Serve God, and join not any partners with Him; and do good—to parents, kinsfolk, orphans, those in need, neighbors who are near, neighbors who are strangers, the companion by your side, the wayfarer (ye meet), and what your right hands possess [the slave]: For God loveth not the arrogant, the vainglorious" (Q:4:36).

We want to think that we follow this rule, yet are we? Would you be upset if someone was polluting the environment that you live in, using up valuable resources for things they don't need, running up debt that you'd have to pay? Yet, that is exactly what we are doing to each other and our children, driven by our entitlement attitudes and actions.

What is the source of this increasing entitlement trend? I believe that there are several sources with some of the big ones being our education system, changing informal social controls around parenting, our obsession with celebrities, and our government-protected economic growth engine with its mind-controlling mass media weapons.

Entitlement is a learned behavior and as such, we need to look at how we raise our children through their formative years to see where it is being introduced. Instead of giving children what they need, parents are now pressured into giving them everything they want. The pressure is intense too. From the billions spent on advertising that is targeted to children, celebrity worship that start trends that our children "have to" follow, social pressure to keep up with the neighbors, and the desire to give our children more than we had, it is no wonder that parents are behaving like they are.

I feel that our education system is also nurturing entitlement in our children with new policies that promote self-esteem and reward participation instead of results. In my opinion, if a student does not hand in an assignment on time, they should get a zero on that assignment. If a student does not meet the minimum standards for a class or grade, they should have to repeat it. Sadly, in many school districts today, this isn't the case. Let me be clear here: In my opinion, the fault lies with the policies that are put in place, not with the teachers.

With our children getting what they want without necessarily putting in the effort to obtain it, both at home and at school, it is little wonder that as they emerge as young adults, they have a great sense of entitlement.

To try and nip entitlement in the bud, I believe that there are several things that parents can do. First, evaluate every purchase and reward that you give your children and ask the tough questions. Do they need this? Did they put in the effort to get it? Did they accomplish what they were supposed to in order to earn it? You can also apply the same principle to yourself. Even though the car companies are saying that you deserve a new vehicle this year, do you really need it and the associated debt?

On the education front we have less influence. Being an active participant though will help. Be aware of assignments that your child has; when possible, review them before they are handed in. Working closely with the teachers and being an active participant with your school board are at least places to start.

Applying this parenting style will, over a period of several decades, hopefully give us a population that overall would feel less entitled. That is if they can avoid the great economic machine that really likes entitlement, especially when it comes to the consumption of things. But even if this new crop of adults can avoid this, will they be around soon enough to make a real difference? In the book *2022*, I went through some of my fears on timelines and my belief is that we don't have decades to wait to start to correct our planet's issues. So, is there anything we can do about the current levels of entitlement?

In order for entitlement to take root, I believe that it must be fueled by an attitude of self-centeredness and self-importance. Therefore, to reduce entitlement, it would seem logical to me that we must change these attitudes. But this isn't an easy task since this would mean that we need to convince individuals that they're just a small part of something bigger, something more important than themselves. Some typical examples of "something bigger" would be a relationship with another person, a community, or a religious faith (an interesting note here is that all of these examples are in a state of decline now).

Overall, I do not see an easy answer here. Yes, working with our children will help, but our current society's level of entitlement is where the real work needs to be done, and it probably will need to be done one person at a time.

APPENDIX B – WHAT DID RICHARD MISS?

"The world will not be destroyed by those that do evil but by those that watch them without doing anything." – Albert Einstein

The rules that Richard laid out when forming the villages did a reasonable job of limiting the entitlement behavior of individuals, but what then? From a behavior standpoint, is it enough to simply be grateful for what we have and to think about others before ourselves?

I guess that may work if the environment we lived in were perfect, if nothing needed improvement, if there was enough of everything for everyone. If this were the case, we could all pursue our own purpose, combining our passions, strengths, values, and service to live rich lives. But this isn't our reality.

Our planet is in a bit of a mess right now. There are a host of issues that need to be addressed, and it is far too easy to become complacent about them—to get used to the way things are and forget that there are things that could or should be done.

In order to avoid this complacency, I feel that we must constantly strive to do more—to set aggressive goals and then work to exceed them. This is what I feel Richard missed when he setup the villages: an enabler for motivation for individuals to make things better.

Let's review the initial set of guidelines that he set out back in 2022.

1. Other than for hunting wildlife, no weapons will be built.
2. Population control will be implemented once a sustainable population has been reached (roughly 2,000).

3.   Allow expansion only if resources are available and if it will cause
      no stress to the environment.
4.   Selective genetic pairing will be done and will be overseen by the
      elders.
5.   Everyone must rotate through all routine tasks in the village for a
      set amount of time as specified by elders.
6.   Everyone must assist in large tasks, such as planting, harvesting,
      building huts, and repairs.
7.   No currency.
8.   No livestock.
9.   No personal possessions other than clothes and what can be
      carried in a backpack.
10.   No elected officials.
11.   No attempts to communicate with the outside world.
12.   Environment is on equal terms with humans.
13.   Each hut will have one elder, and the elder's word is law for the
      hut. Each elder will select a successor who cannot be a direct
      descendant.
14.   One of the elders will also be the leader for the village and his or
      her word will be law. The leader will select his or her successor,
      again someone who is not a direct descendant.
15.   An elder or the village leader can be replaced only if the vast
      majority of the other elders agree.

All of these guidelines work towards reducing entitlement and taking better
care of the planet. What I believe is missing are these two guidelines:

16.   Once per year, the elders will determine two or three goals for
      activities that will improve either the community or the planet. One
      of the clan hut elders will be assigned to each goal and will be
      responsible for coordinating tasks around it and reporting back
      progress.

17.   Once per year, each individual six years and older will declare an
      activity that they'll do that aligns with the goals laid out by the
      elders.

What is the purpose of these two new guidelines? The first one identifies issues that need to be addressed, usually at the leader level since at the individual level it is not always obvious where the real problems are. It also serves to focus the entire community to work together to a common end. The second one ensures that the individual defines an actionable activity that is in alignment with the group's direction.

Relating these guidelines to our real world, I feel that our leaders must take a much more active role in setting goals and outlining actions that can be done to achieve these goals. Perhaps we, as individuals, have become too complacent in this area; we don't expect our leaders to lead and to set goals. Perhaps individuals need to take a more active role in challenging our leaders to do more. For instance, challenging them to list their top three goals for reducing our impact on the planet, what they are doing about it, and suggestions on what we as individuals can do as well.

In the world today, I feel that many of us are too complacent about many points that I have brought up in the Percipience series. Take for example the simple act of recycling aluminum beverage cans. In 2013 in the United States, one third of these cans were **not** recycled. Bottled water is even worse with only roughly thirty percent of the bottles being recycled in the United States.

Much of the driver behind complacency is that we get into routines. We get in the habit of doing or seeing something and then we do not think about how it could be improved because it does not impact us directly. I feel that we must constantly challenge ourselves to improve in all areas of our lives. This includes the way we treat our planet, interact with others, the way we work, and what we learn.

APPENDIX C – WHAT'S NEXT?

"What do you think you'd like to be when you grow up?"
Charlie Brown asked.
"Outrageously happy," Linus replied.

Charles M. Schulz, In January 1960 Peanuts *comic strip*

Throughout this series, I've laid out my viewpoint and fears for where we are heading—a future that we or a generation or so from now will experience. It appears that it will not be pleasant unless some serious action is taken now.

So the question is what is next? As I've stated earlier, I don't have faith that our leaders will react in time to make any appreciable difference. This leaves us at the individual level—you and me. The only practical solution that I see to this is for each of us to muster up the courage to seriously look at ourselves and ask the tough questions.

1. What is my current level of entitlement?
2. Are there areas where I have become complacent?
3. Do I care enough to change?
4. What actionable items can I do right now?
5. Can I be open about this to friends in hopes to both inform and get them engaged as well?

With today's level of technology in the area of communication, a few people can make a difference. Through social media, blogs, and other methods, a broad group of people can be reached to make them aware of the issues and give them suggestions on what they can do about it.

Another avenue for support is our faith. While there are many differences in the major religions, one thing that is common amongst all of them is that we are part of something bigger, and religion does not advocate the entitlement virus that has infected our population. Perhaps we can leverage this to get the "drastically reduce consumption and care more for others" message out.

As for the Percipience book series, I'm going to let Lauren, Alec, Clyde, and Heather take a break while I go and find out where and when Richard went. I'm pretty passionate on the underlying subject of sustainability though and will continue to write on it through my website www.the2222book.com

All Feedback, either through my website or through a review/rating on Amazon, Goodreads or Librarything is greatly appreciated.

2232

Proof

Made in the USA
Charleston, SC
29 September 2015